THE TROLL-TROLL WAR

THE TROLL WARS TRILOGY: BOOK THREE

LEAH R CUTTER

KNOTTED ROAD PRESS

The Troll-Troll War
The Troll Wars Trilogy: Book Three
Copyright © 2019 Leah Cutter
All rights reserved
Published by Knotted Road Press
www.KnottedRoadPress.com

ISBN: 978-1-64470-043-3

Cover Art:
ID 21987573 © Prometeus | Depositphoto.com

Cover and interior design copyright © 2019 Knotted Road Press
http://www.KnottedRoadPress.com

Come someplace new…
If you'd like to be notified of new releases, sign up for my newsletter.

I will never spam you or use your email for nefarious purposes. You can also unsubscribe at any time.

http://www.LeahCutter.com/newsletter/

ALSO BY LEAH R CUTTER

Seattle Trolls

The Changeling Troll

The Princess Troll

The Fairy-Bridge Troll

The Troll-Demon War

The Troll-Human War

The Troll-Troll War

The Cassie Stories

Poisoned Pearls

Tainted Waters

Spoiled Harvest

Bloodied Ice

Tanish Empire Trilogy

The Glass Magician

The Desert Heart

The Ghost Dog

The Shadow Wars Trilogy

The Raven and the Dancing Tiger

The Guardian Hound

War Among the Crocodiles

The Clockwork Fairy Kingdom

The Clockwork Fairy Kingdom

The Maker, the Teacher, and the Monster

The Dwarven Wars

The Chronicles of Franklin

Franklin Versus The Popcorn Thief

Franklin Versus The Soul Thief

Franklin Versus The Child Thief

Contemporary Fantasy

Siren's Call

The Immortals' War

Circle of Air

CHAPTER ONE

KING GARETHEN KEPT A SMILE PLASTERED TO HIS face as he raised his glass to the most recent toast of Princess Kizalynn. He sat with two dozen trolls from the court in one of the great halls, the remains of their stupendous feast scattered across the long table in front of them: wild boar with the first apples of the season, more tart than sweet; hearty bacon-onion soup that had a marvelous tang from the aged cheese melted into it; as well as a dozen more delicacies that the chefs had plied the table with, their own form of celebration.

The hall itself echoed with the voices of jubilant trolls as they drank and toasted the princess, the king, as well as their fallen warriors. The feast had been a spontaneous event, so the trolls merely wore their court finery, and were primarily dressed in jewel tones: emerald greens, sapphire blues, ruby reds, with lots of gold.

Garethen wore a sleeveless red tunic with a design of branches and leaves stitched in gold thread across the chest, along with finely made black wool pants that ended just below the knee and comfortable black leather shoes. He'd kept his heavy gold crown on for the celebration, weighing down his long white hair. Years before, he'd considered adding gold caps to his tusks, but they'd be merely decorative and he couldn't see the need. Besides, he always felt that his tusks, yellowed with age, gave him a certain dignity. It was why he generally wore sleeveless tunics, not only to show his court that he was still very muscular and could defeat any of them in hand-to-hand combat, but also to show his battle scars, that he'd earned his place among them.

Along the walls, tapestries hung from the ceiling to the floor, commemorating other battles the trolls had won, along with a few that were more whimsical and illustrated myths, like the troll princess in the tower and the great hero troll flinging stones at the moon.

Garethen knew he needed to let the court be for the time being, to let them have their celebration, though he wanted to yell and shake his fist at all of them.

They had not won the Great War. Just a great battle. There were too many of the *kith and kin* who had allied themselves with the demons, too many demons who hadn't been at the battle and who still desperately fought on, too many unknowns.

Besides, if Garethen let himself believe that they'd already won the war, he would start grinding his teeth and growling about all the gold that he'd spent. If he'd just waited a couple of weeks before giving the royal treasurer Phikathera his extra chests of gold, maybe he would have been able to keep them.

It just wasn't fair. The hole in his secret closet where he

kept the gold, where those two chests had sat, gnawed at him. His mind kept circling back to them, probing that empty space, wishing to fill it again.

And Phikathera hadn't let him raise taxes again. So that hole was unlikely to be filled soon.

It took Garethen a moment to realize that someone had addressed him directly.

"Sorry," Garethen said, taking another sip of his very fine dark beer. "Just wool gathering. What did you ask?"

The young male—Ezekielan—gave the king a knowing smile. "I understand. Matters of state and like that." He paused, then asked again, "Do you know when the princess is likely to visit? So that we may honor her in person?"

Garethen replied blandly, "She still has a war to fight. She'll come home when she can." He suspected he knew the real reason for Ezekielan's request. He was a young troll, the son of Lord Ra'mok, and was probably angling to ask for Kizalynn's hand in marriage.

"I see," Ezekielan said thoughtfully. He lowered his voice so that Garethen had to listen carefully to hear his next question. "What do you think our chances are? Of actually winning?"

Garethen raised his eyebrows in surprise. Seemed that Ezekielan had a good head on his shoulders and hadn't been carried away with the rest of his court by the good news about the battle.

He gave Ezekielan an appraising look. The boy was handsome enough for a troll, though his nose looked as though he'd broken it at one point and not had it set straight. His right lower tusk had a gouge in it as well.

Ezekielan wore a dark green long-sleeved shirt under a finely made black vest, so Garethen couldn't see if the young man had battle scars. Ezekielan was quite muscular though, particularly for someone in the court.

"I rate our chances at better than fifty-fifty," Garethen finally replied. "Higher if we can win a few more decisive battles in the next few days."

"I see," Ezekielan said, his dark brown eyes somber. "I'm certain that you've provided Princess Kizalynn with all that she needs in order to succeed. But if there's ever anything else, make sure you let the court know."

"I will," Garethen said. "Thank you. I appreciate that."

Ezekielan raised his glass in a silent toast to his king before turning away to chat with his neighbor again.

Interesting. Seemed as though there were some thinkers in among the courtiers.

Would Kizalynn be attracted to this Ezekielan? Garethen was going to have to do some checking into the young troll's background to see if he would be a suitable match.

Not that Garethen planned on abdicating the throne anytime soon. No, he wanted to bask in the praise and rewards sure to come his way as a result of Kizalynn leading the troops successfully.

But maybe once she was married off, he could think about stepping down.

Though if he did it sooner, then maybe he wouldn't have to spend more of the gold he'd accumulated. It would be *his*, and his alone. Kizalynn would just have to figure out how to finance her reign herself.

Though maybe Phikathera would allow Garethen to

tax the court to help pay for the war effort. If he could get someone like Ezekielan to plead his case for him among them…

It was worth considering.

Garethen found his smile growing, a real smile this time.

Yes, maybe he could turn a profit and replace the gold from his chests sooner rather than later.

CHAPTER TWO

CHRISTINE TUCKERMAN, A.K.A. PRINCESS KIZALYNN Linumok Te'Dur, carefully stepped through the portal into the king's palace. She had her great ax in her hands and wore what she considered her dress uniform. It was similar to what the king's guard wore, with massive rings of metal sewn into a navy blue sleeveless tunic, pants cropped just below her knee, and tall black boots. She wore her peaked helmet—gold instead of the guard's silver—with spaces for her tall ears cut out on either side.

The first attack was a mighty wind, strong enough to push an average troll back through the portal, or at least hold her against the wall until enough guards could be summoned.

Christine's own air elemental defended her, blowing out from her chest and forcing the gale winds to curve and howl around her.

Next, the huge vats of burning rocks which hung near the ceiling turned and emptied their contents onto her. Christine's fire elemental leaped up to burn away the lava-like stones before they even touched her. They landed with soft thuds around her feet, merely smoking coals.

Christine scurried forward, reaching for the stones beside the doorway. Her hand instinctively found the spot where her palm print had been carved out.

Before the next trap could be released, Christine called forth the royal sigil buried deep in the stones surrounding the door to the portal room. The lopsided treble clefs filled the room with blue light as they rose, neutralizing the rest of the traps.

Christine sighed as she slipped her great ax onto her back, then looked around. Her air element automatically brought her jewel-colored lights, like the human Christmas tree lights, across the tops of all the walls.

The damage wasn't too bad this time. Christine was never certain what order the traps would come in. Ozlandia, the head of the king's guard, said that was to keep Christine on her toes.

Christine took the time to refill the vats with burning rock, as well as close off the wind tunnels before she opened the door to the portal room.

A guard just outside stood at attention. She knew she'd been introduced to him at one point, though she couldn't remember his name. Balanidaro perhaps? A second guard stood down the hallway, poised to run and raise the alarm if whoever came through the door was not Christine.

"Pumpkin pie," Christine announced in Trollish. She was still quite proud of the fact that she could now speak her native tongue. Not quite like a native, but close enough.

The guard nearest the door gave her a broad smile. "With good whipped cream, your highness," he replied, finishing the password that had been set. "Are you here to see the king?"

"I am," Christine said. She dreaded confronting Garethen about the cambion demons crossing the fairy bridge. However, she wasn't about to put it off. She'd waited until after lunch, though, as the king would likely be alone in his study at this point.

The guard at the end of the hallway came closer. "I'll trade ye," he said.

He was a younger guard, one who Christine didn't think she'd met yet. Still, he wore his uniform proudly, and took up the first guard's place at the door with a stiff back and a wide grin.

"Your name's Balanidaro, right?" Christine asked the guard walking beside her.

Balanidaro beamed at her. "Yes, my lady." He seemed even more full of pride that she'd remembered his name.

"Got the short end of the shift?" Christine said.

"Don't know what you mean, my lady."

"Guarding an empty hallway for hours on end can't be a choice station."

"Well, maybe, sometimes," Balanidaro said with a sly grin. "However, when we know there's a good chance you'll be coming, it's a much more sought after gig."

"Good to know," Christine said.

They passed not one, but two heavy rock doors that could be used to close off the hallway leading to the portal room. Ozlandia took the security of the palace very seriously. Christine had had to work much harder to convince her that a portal room could be made safe—the king had agreed to the plan almost immediately.

Once Christine and Balanidaro passed the second rock door, they were into the regular part of the palace. The walls were whitewashed here to make it brighter, and thick rugs covered the smooth, stone floor, giving the rooms a homey feeling. Sconces holding clay oil lamps hung at regular intervals, burning without smoke while still adding a nice spicy scent to the air.

Balanidaro automatically took them on a circuitous way through the palace, passing through long banquet halls and dusty passageways, instead of the main hallways. It wasn't that Christine didn't want to see anyone. She knew, however, that every troll she met would spend their time congratulating her on her big victory and she'd never have time to actually see the king.

When they reached the outside of the king's study, a single guard stood there. Her eyes grew big when she saw who Balanidaro was escorting.

"He's—he's not here," she stammered. "Feast," she managed to get out next.

"Ah, right," Balanidaro said, turning. "This way."

"Wait a second," Christine said, thinking furiously. "This was only supposed to be a short visit. To consult with the king," she added. If she went to the hall where the troll court was feasting, she might not get out of there for hours. Plus, she still would need to confront the king afterward.

"Not a social call, then," Balanidaro said slowly.

Christine came to a decision. "I know you're not a messenger. Still, could you please go and let the king know that I'm here? Waiting for him in his study? Without alerting the rest of the court?" She didn't know if she could count on Balanidaro's discretion. Trolls weren't necessarily subtle.

Balanidaro's eyes grew wide. "Yes, my lady. You can count on me." He turned to the younger female guard standing outside the king's study. "Not a word. Not even a hint to anyone what you just heard. Understand?"

The younger troll gulped. "Yes, sir. My lady," she said, nodding at Christine.

"I'll let Peticurian know as well, outside the portal room," Balanidaro assured Christine.

"Thank you," Christine said, impressed. Seemed that Balanidaro was trustworthy.

She let herself into the king's study to wait. She liked this room, felt comfortable here. Someday, she'd set herself up with a similar room in the palace. Christine appreciated the trollish approach to architecture, which meant merely thin slits for windows were cut into the solid stone walls instead of huge, human-style windows. Much better to be surrounded by good rock.

Behind the king's desk hung a beautiful purple geode, about three feet in diameter. Christine approved of that. However, no books were held in the cases that lined the other walls. There were some pretty stones there, more geodes, and a few scrolls. Her study, on the other hand, would have lots of books.

She also liked his desk, which had been shaped out of a single boulder of granite. She might have something similar, but possibly not. She'd been raised as a human, and so wood didn't bother her as much. A single notebook sat on the corner of the desk, where the king took notes now and again to jog his memory of things.

Was his promise to the demons also recorded there? Christine wouldn't violate his privacy by checking, despite being curious.

The king's chair, as well as the two guest chairs on the other side of the desk, were all made out of iron with dark green leather cushions. Christine sat herself in one of those.

She didn't have to wait for long. The king came bursting into the room after just a short time.

"Ah, daughter!" King Garethen said, holding out his hands to her. They didn't embrace, but they did clasp arms, like soldiers did. "So good to see you!"

Christine plastered a big smile on her face and nodded, saying, "It's good to see you," while at the same time studying the king closely.

She couldn't see the demonic influence. No one could. If she was being fanciful, she'd say that it was there in the corners of his eyes, which were now a touch beady, instead of holding the wide sincere look of most trolls.

"What's wrong?" the king asked, noting her study of him.

Christine nodded, letting her smile slip. "We have to talk," she said.

CHAPTER THREE

Lars Sorgenfreys angrily paced across barren rock in the pocket world he'd escaped to. He wore his demon form. The winds were only strong enough to flutter the tattered black leather that hung from the bone struts that made up his huge wings. His powerful legs pulverized the smaller rocks in his path as he stomped back and forth. Black ichor dripped from his long forked tongue, spattering and hissing when it struck the ground. The yellowish scales on his chest gave off a pale light despite the overcast sky—Lars assumed the light was fueled by his righteous rage.

The other creatures on this plane—minor demons who held their allegiance to Lars and his family—stayed the hell away from him as he fumed. They cavorted instead in the mists that gathered just off the edges of the cliffs, too stupid to realize that it wasn't necessarily a great honor that Lars had stopped off here.

What had gone wrong? How had Lars been tricked?

While most demons would have blamed someone,

anyone, other than themselves for their defeat, Lars held himself firmly accountable.

That damned troll Christine had tricked him. Lars was a big enough demon to almost, *almost*, admire that in an enemy. Particularly a stupid troll who shouldn't have been smart enough to pull off such a feat.

Then again, it hadn't just been Christine in on the trick. Her human doppelganger, Tina, had played a huge part.

Maybe that was Lars' problem. He'd been too focused on Christine and had stopped paying enough attention to Tina. Then again, Tina had been so thoroughly corrupted and influenced by demons that he shouldn't have had to worry about her.

How had she broken free of his influence? Should he try to corrupt her again? Or did he need to focus his attention elsewhere?

He needed to come up with a new plan. Now. It was what he was known for. It was how he'd gotten so far in his plans for the war. He'd had contingency plans for dealing with the small, miniscule chance that his grand encounter with Christine had ended in a failure.

None of them had dealt with the loss of the corruption crystals.

So now, Lars was starting at square one. He needed to rally his troops, carry them forward despite the minor defeat. Demons *hated* losing more than anything else.

Lars knew he didn't have much time to plan. Beelzebub (known as Buddy to his friends) had granted Lars the use of four armies with which to start the Great War in exchange for Lars' soul. If Buddy and the other princes of Hell decided that Lars had well and truly lost the Great War, Lars' soul was forfeit.

He just had to come up with his next great plan in less than an hour, instead of taking five years to craft it.

A presence impinged on Lars' consciousness. Someone was trying to get his attention.

At first, Lars ignored them. It was probably a messenger from Buddy, demanding Lars' presence down in Hell to explain himself and what had happened.

Lars could only put Buddy and the other princes of Hell off for so long. He'd have to report eventually.

He needed a plan before then.

After the third tiresome ping and getting no closer to his goal, Lars finally focused on the demon who was trying to get his attention.

Huh. It wasn't one of Buddy's minions. Instead, it was the cambion Lars had hired to help him corrupt the king of the trolls.

Surprised, Lars answered the call, allowing Manny the cambion access to the pocket world.

"Oh! My supreme leader! My glorious combatant! Long live your unholy rule!" Manny proclaimed as he stepped onto the rocks.

Lars tried not to roll his eyes too hard. Manny, like the other cambions, was a suckup. Came from their mixed heritage, being part human and not a full-fledged demon.

Manny wasn't that ugly as a demon, though he did make a hideous human. The placement of his wide-set eyes gave him the look of a cow that all the brains had been bred out of. His long nose ran constantly with a thick yellow snot. The few patches of hair that stuck out of his mostly bare skull were long and greasy.

At least he had proper demon eyes, black with a touch of the abyss lurking in the depths. His claws did leave much to be desired, despite having six fingers and four toes. He wore human style clothing—a filth-encrusted blue vest that strained across his extended belly, and torn wool pants held around his waist with a rope belt.

"What news do you have?" Lars said in a bored tone, as if he hadn't been frantically trying to plan his next move. "You said it was important."

"It is! It is!" Manny said, nodding and rocking back and forth on his stubby feet.

Lars made a "go on" motion, already regretting that he'd allowed Manny access at this time.

"Oh! Right! Well, the thing is, Christine and a mighty powerful magician killed a dozen of my people last night," Manny said. "In the human plane. It was a horrible slaughter. Innocent demons slain, their lives abruptly ended, the carnage—"

"So?" Lars interrupted. He didn't see the relevance. "Lots of demons die in war." He'd just had huge swaths of his own armies killed by that damned obelisk of truth.

"So, my great lord, as you may recall, I had weaseled a promise from the king of the trolls to grant us safe passage," Manny said, puffing up his chest with pride. "I know you appreciate how much gold that cost us," he added.

What, did this pipsqueak honestly think that Lars was about to pay him back? This was war. Fortunes were frequently lost as a consequence.

"And?" Lars said when Manny didn't go on.

"It's the first time the princess troll has bothered us. I don't know for sure, but my impression was that she didn't even know we were crossing the bridge," Manny said. "I thought it was important that you should know the actions of our enemy, as soon as they occurred. It was such a tremendous blow to your glorious plan of sneaking as many demons across the various borders as possible. Now, the fairy bridge is less open, less responsive."

"Wait a second," Lars said. "Back up. She didn't bother you before last night?"

"Not once," Manny said. "Don't think she knew," he repeated.

Huh. This might actually be the information Lars needed. His mind started spinning out plans and traps, how he could use this to his advantage and still win the Great War.

After a few moments, Manny cleared his throat.

"Oh. You're still here?" Lars said, distracted. "You're dismissed."

"Thank you, my unholy liege, for allowing me to contribute even the smallest part to your great war effort," Manny said, backing away. "Let me know if there's ever anything else you need from me or my race. We look forward to serving our full demon overlords."

Lars knew that Manny was angling for a reward for having come forward with the news he'd brought.

"And see my treasurer for a reward," Lars added grudgingly. He didn't have a magical, unending supply of gold to fund the war. However, he knew he needed to give this cambion a bonus. Now that Lars thought about it,

Manny was the closest demon he had to the troll king. It was better to keep Manny fat and happy, as it were, to skewer him and roast him slowly later.

"Oh, thank you, my liege! Thank you!" Manny said backing away more quickly now, aware that Lars could change his mind any moment.

After Manny had stepped through the portal, Lars started pacing again. This was no longer the angry step of the desperate. Instead, Lars practically bounced as he walked along, the plan coming together beautifully.

Many of the *kith and kin* races had already folded, realigning themselves with their natural masters, the demons. And not every demon had swallowed a corruption crystal, even though they'd sworn that they had. Huge portions of the demon armies had merely been carrying them, and so hadn't really been injured. They'd only received superficial burns when the crystals had exploded.

If that damned princess troll pressed her advantage right now, hard, Lars and his armies might have to give way. He'd lose ground. He might have to admit defeat.

However, if Christine was distracted, say, by a civil war among the trolls…

Lars couldn't help but give an evil cackle. He'd have to get Manny to apply more pressure to the king. As well as see just how far his influence spread among the other trolls in the court.

Yes. If he could get Christine to take her eye off the ball, the demons could win the Great War yet.

CHAPTER FOUR

Tina stepped cautiously into the pocket space where she used to practice her magic. Her bio-dad, Vern, stood beside her. They were both in casual clothes, T-shirts and jeans, and barefoot. (Tina was so happy to have at least one person who was magical understand that shoes just constricted the flow of magic.)

At one point, Tina had been most comfortable here, in her practice room. She'd colored the walls the soothing green of new grass, then applied a pattern of curling white strips, like wind blowing fresh air. Gray padded cushions covered the floor, so Tina could sit or stand for ages and not be tired or sore.

If Tina hadn't been paying close attention to the walls as she came in, she might have been fooled. The illusion of purity that the demonic corruption crystals cast was still strong.

Finally, though, she was well enough that she could see how nasty and *influenced* her space had become. The demons had been able to sneak around the pockets of space that humans had carved out, piling corruption crystals on the other side of the wall.

Now, she saw what looked like black mold covering the walls. It had started in the far corner and crept over all the surfaces. She could even smell it, a scent like wet, rotting drywall.

She looked over at Vern, who had a grim expression on his face. It was unusual seeing him look that way. She'd always thought of him as Christine's goofy dad. Okay, so he still was kind of goofy.

Gaining magic had changed him. As had going and actually fighting demons. Just a small battle, and Christine had told Tina that she'd actually taken care of most of the demons for Vern.

He'd still waded in and gotten his wand bloody. Christine had sworn that it had been necessary for him to feel as though he was doing something for the war, even though he'd run away from the great battle itself.

"Kind of skanky," Vern declared, looking around. "No offense."

"None taken," Tina said. She took a deep breath and found that she was shaking.

She needed to either clean her practice place and get rid of every single tiny bit of demonic influence, or else destroy the place and build a new one. She could see the advantages to both.

Her adoptive parents, the Zimmermans, had advocated for her to just get rid of the old place. It would take a lot of time and effort for her to clean this place. Plus, it was common knowledge that most magical items couldn't be trusted after they'd been cleansed. Demons could corrupt them again too easily.

However, both Vern as well as her old teacher Malcom had advised Tina to first try to clean her practice room. It would help her healing process to tackle such a job and make good headway. It would possibly also help her own natural defenses against demonic influence.

Tina felt the familiar black hopelessness brushing up against her as she looked around. What was the point? Even if she got this place clean, she'd never return to it. She couldn't trust it. She couldn't trust herself to actually purify the space.

She glanced at Vern, who told her, "Your call. Still think you'd feel better if you could whip some demonic butt. It made me feel better," he assured her, giving her a weak smile. "Got my groove back."

Tina knew that Vern was putting on something of a brave face. He'd been shaken by killing demons with Christine on the human side of the fairy bridge.

It finally occurred to her that possibly this would be good for Vern as well, to clean out a corrupted space.

Tina and Vern had spent some time together after they'd discovered that she was his biological daughter. Not a lot of time, and not because Vern hadn't tried, but because Tina had felt uncomfortable. Guilty as well, for how her adoptive parents had treated Christine. Tina kept expecting Vern and Lizzie to get angry with her, to blame her for part of it.

They'd remained supportive, however, not only of her but of their troll daughter.

Tina consciously recalled the bright day they'd left

behind, how beautiful the late September weather had been, how pretty the trees were with their fall colors.

Then she brought her magic back up inside of her. It still bubbled and made her glow. But the light was no longer pure white. Instead, it felt more like tempered gold.

Vern gave her a big grin and drew out his wand. She'd never seen one like his before. Instead of the traditional wood, it was made from blue resin with gold flecks swimming through the material. She'd thought it was weird at first. It looked so natural in his hand, as if it had been made for him.

She considered her own wand, feeling the nobs on the wood. Huh. She hadn't liked this wand as much as her old, corrupt one. Maybe it wasn't because she wasn't used to it, but because it wasn't the right material.

She'd have to think about that. Maybe Vern would go wand shopping with her sometime.

In the meanwhile, they had a room to clean.

No one had discovered the perfect spell to deal with the corruption crystals the demons had created. The obelisk of truth had destroyed them in the single battle, then the pieces of it had separated and disappeared again, until the next time of great need.

While Tina could scrub the walls of her practice room clean, she had to get at the source of the contamination, the crystals piled up against the other side. She'd tried expanding the walls of her space to bring the crystals inside the room, but she'd only succeeded in pushing the walls out, not moving them to capture what was lurking outside.

That meant that every time Tina and Vern cleaned a wall and turned their attention elsewhere, when they turned back to the once purified wall, black spots of corruption had returned.

Tina did have to admit that Vern and Malcom had been correct—it had felt good cleaning this space as much as they could. It had reminded her how powerful she actually was. It had also felt good to have some bio-dad time.

However, her failure gnawed at her.

Tina and Vern sat on the floor, leaning their backs up against the wall opposite where most of the crystals had been placed. Every time a black dot showed up, either Vern or Tina would zap it with magic.

"Do you think you could make a portal into the empty space?" Vern asked, tossing yet another idea out for how they could get at the crystals so that they could destroy them.

Tina shook her head. "You can only create a portal to someplace else that you've already been to," she said. "And the empty space is in between spaces. I don't how to get there."

Vern nodded thoughtfully. "Could you make the walls here transparent? So you could see into the other space?"

Tina took a deep breath and thought for a moment. "Possibly. But I'm not sure that's wise. I've been told that it's an abyss. Looking into it is likely to drive a human insane."

Vern snorted. "So it's a kind of demonic place, then?" he asked. "A chaotic, comfortable place for them?"

"Maybe," Tina said. She didn't like thinking that one of the things that she did most naturally actually involved brushing against something so impure.

It was one of the things that made Vern rare. Most people came into their magic as kids, so they'd been trained in it since they were young. Vern was older and brought more of an adult's perspective and questioning of things, instead of accepting everything as it was presented.

"So do we call it a day for now?" Vern asked quietly. "Go and do some more research then come back?"

It made Tina smile despite how she didn't want to give up. At least Vern hadn't asked her to destroy her room. He understood that she still loved this place, despite how wrecked and spoiled it was.

"That might be for the best," Tina admitted, zapping the next black spot that appeared on the wall opposite them.

Vern nodded and pushed himself up to standing, moving more stiffly than she'd thought he would—she kept thinking of him as younger than he was. He held out his hand to her, to help her stand as well.

Tina took Vern's hard hand in hers. Though he didn't look that strong, his hands struck her as being very muscular. Though neither of them liked touching anyone casually, it just seemed right for her to take her bio-dad's hand for a moment, to let his strength flow into her.

"I'm going to try one last thing," Tina said. Vern nodded and took a step back, giving her space to shine.

Tina mustered every bit of power that she had. When

she'd been under demonic influence, she'd tapped into some very dark powers. Using them could corrupts her. It was dicey to use them, even the slightest bit. However, it was too tempting not to try.

She blasted the far wall with the strongest purity spell she could manage. It bleached the green out of the wall, turning it stark white. Tina continued to pour on the power. The wall vibrated under the attack.

On the other side of the wall, Tina felt the corruption crystals, like tiny burrs, prickly. She burned off the edges of them with her light and her power.

Darkness came welling back up inside of herself, called to by the darkness she was striving against. She pushed it back down, the stream weakening.

There were too many of the corruption crystals on the far side of the wall. A pile of them, maybe two feet tall and three feet across.

She destroyed the smaller crystals scattered at the base of the other walls, where just one or two have been placed.

The bigger pile was going to take a lot more effort and strength than she had, if she only used the cleaner portions of her power.

"I think you did it!" Vern declared as Tina dropped her hands and stepped back. Her arms shook and her knees felt weak. A whisper of the darkness inside her blew through her core. If only she'd give in.

"No," Tina said softly, addressing both Vern as well as the parts inside of her. She'd burned out a few of the crystals. Not all of them. Plus, the demons were likely to come back and replace the ones she'd destroyed.

No, she needed to come up with a permanent solution.

She took a deep breath and firmly squashed the darkness that had oh so easily welled up inside her. She had to figure out how to deal with that as well. Just ignoring it had worked temporarily.

Those voices would always be there, tempting her. And she'd give in. She needed a better solution for that as well.

Vern and Tina left the practice room through the portal Vern proudly created. Tina couldn't help but smile at his joy.

However, in her mind's eye, she saw the pretty walls of her practice room start slowly become corrupted again, the black dots appearing and spreading across the walls.

Could she save it? Should she? And how could she continue to defend herself against the dark powers that were all too easy to tap within herself?

CHAPTER FIVE

BUDDY SAT ON HIS THRONE MADE OF IRON CASTS OF the skulls of his enemies and waited while Lars went on and on and *on* about his new plans, how he intended to still lead the demons to victory.

They were alone in the throne room. Buddy had never gotten around to redoing the design, so it still had red glowing rocks that spewed lava when Buddy lost his temper, walls specifically carved so that any unwary who brushed against them would be sliced by the sharp stones, and a plain rock floor that was magically hardened so that even the most caustic of demonic fluids wouldn't eat through it.

Buddy idly scratched at his potbelly, listening to Lars with half an ear. Should he call a halt to Lars' rant? The younger demon said he had a point. It wasn't time for lunch yet, was it? Buddy's stomach rumbled at the thought.

Was Buddy going to have to go into full demon mode to get Lars to get to the point? Generally, Buddy appeared mostly harmless, particularly for a prince of Hell. He had floppy ears that gave him a porcine appearance, a long nose with yet another annoying infected sore along the side of it, and flabby lips that hid strong, sharp teeth that were well suited for tearing either flesh or souls to shreds. Buddy preferred that his fellow demons underestimate him, but he felt as though his good nature was being abused by Lars.

"Enough!" Buddy roared as he swung his legs from where they'd been resting across one of the arms of the throne. He stood up on his bare feet, keeping his mostly harmless form. "I've had enough of your plans," he growled. "Tell me what happened."

Lars blinked at him. It almost made Buddy smile to see the shock in the young demon's face.

Almost.

"I underestimated my enemy," Lars said.

Buddy blinked, surprised at any demon admitting fault. "You what?"

Lars shrugged. "I lost a battle," he said casually, as if he was discussing the tacos he'd just had for lunch.

Demons did not do that. Had Lars somehow been infected with goodness? How was that even possible?

"However, I have *not* lost the Great War," Lars insisted. "That damned princess troll hasn't defeated me. It was a single defeat. Plus, she's about to be distracted by a civil war among the trolls."

"Interesting," Buddy said. He had to hand it to the boy—he really did plan well. "How will you manage a civil war?" He held up his hand to forestall yet *another* long, complicated spiel. Really, Lars should think about writing for politicians someday. "The short version," Buddy insisted.

Lars nodded, collecting his thoughts. "I have corrupted the king of the trolls. He's granted safe passage to the cambion demons across the fairy bridge. The bridge that Christine controls."

"Won't she just kill him?" Buddy asked. That was how inheritance was often settled, not only by humans but frequently by the other races of the *kith and kin.*

"She's too soft," Lars said. "Plus, even if she does kill him outright, the rest of the trolls won't follow her. Particularly not the court. I have many hooks in them as well."

"So even if she whips your ass again, she can't hold the territory she takes back because she'll no longer have any support from home," Buddy said.

Buddy snorted at Lars' shocked expression. "You aren't the only one who can see these things, you know," he said, anger tinging his words.

Lars visibly gulped.

Huh. Maybe Buddy was more angry than he realized. He shrank back down to his usual potbellied self.

"Of course *you* can see the cause and effect," Lars said. "You're a prince of Hell, much smarter than the common demons I've been dealing with."

Buddy had to agree to that. He knew the types of generals Lars had, ones who wouldn't show too much ambition or initiative. "That's why I'm the Ultimate General," Buddy reminded Lars, just to watch the boy grind his teeth. He was merely the Supreme General.

"What do you need from me in order to complete the

Great War?" Buddy asked. There wasn't any guarantee that he'd give Lars, well, anything except a quick shiv in the back. He still felt it was his role to ask such questions.

Normally, a demon would be digging into his superior for every ounce of gold he could get. So it surprised Buddy when Lars merely shook his head and said, "Nothing for the moment. I need to reorganize the troops. We've been successful so far because of the corruption crystals, but not a single self-respecting demon will carry those, now. So the mixture of magic users and physical fighters has to change."

Buddy nodded. He hadn't thought about that himself, but it sounded like a good plan. "Where will you attack next?" he asked.

Lars thought for a moment, then nodded. "The rowdy boys' world."

"Again?" Buddy asked, aghast. "Wasn't that where you were just defeated?"

"By a magical device that's long since disappeared," Lars pointed out. "They won't be expecting another attack so soon. Their defenses will be down. And Christine will be too preoccupied to help."

Buddy wasn't sure it would work. But if any demon could come back from such a defeat, it would be Lars.

"Then I'll let you get back to your armies," Buddy said, not bothering to invite Lars to lunch. Never mind the fact that Buddy had made Lars cool his heels outside the throne room for at least half an hour before calling him in.

"Thank you, uh, Ultimate General," Lars said. He

didn't bow—demons didn't bow. He still nodded sharply before he marched away.

Maybe Buddy should insist that Lars salute him next time? Or would Buddy have to return the salute? He'd have to think about that.

In the meanwhile, surely there were tacos to be had. Buddy had to fortify himself before his next meeting. He still kept Curly, one of Lars' primary generals, on his payroll. The demon who Lars was most likely to be attracted to, once she changed her voice. The one who would gladly act as a black widow, killing Lars after he won the Great War.

She'd been insisting on showing Buddy her seduction tricks, looking for pointers on how to influence such a strong demon. Buddy was more than happy to show her.

So yes, fortification. Then he'd meet with Curly and make sure she would be ready with her knife when Lars was least expecting it.

CHAPTER SIX

Ty Brooks, demon hunter extraordinaire, woke with a start, already half transformed from his human form into part wolf. He sat up on his bed and looked around his tiny apartment, sniffing and listening.

Outside the first-story window, he heard the morning buses and frustrated commuters in their cars, trying to get off Capitol Hill and to their respective places of employment. He smelled the lovely leftover ribeye that he'd had for dinner the night before, served with garlic mashed potatoes and cheesy broccoli. As well as the heavenly stout that had served as good as any dessert.

The parquet wooden floor still looked clean, not covered in the ashes that he still vaguely remembered from his dreams. The tiny kitchen was also spotless, as Ty generally always ate out. The piece of equipment he used most often was the microwave, heating up leftovers.

Why was he still so unnerved? What was bothering him? It had just been a dream, right?

Ty's mother had been a full werewolf, while his father

had been human. His dad had insisted that Ty go through a strict training regimen as a child, supplemented with plenty of meditation, so that Ty could transform at will.

Most of the other lycanthropes that Ty knew considered him an abomination because he could control the monster inside of him.

He considered them just as bad, chaining their children to an unending cycle they had no control over.

Ty hadn't had issues with his training since he'd been a teenager. (Hormones had been a real bitch.) He'd lived to tell about it.

Why was he suddenly so on edge? It didn't make any sense.

Ty made himself get up out of bed, putting his feet on the cool floor. He wore only a T-shirt and boxer-briefs to sleep in. The room had a definite fall chill. He could scent the marine layer that still coated the city.

After a few more deep breaths, Ty planted his feet and centered himself. He bowed to the northern corner of his room, then started his own form of Tai Chi. It closely resembled the one he'd been taught as a child, though he'd adapted it to be a fighting form for someone who had half-turned, part human, part wolf. So it contained more slashes, more bites, and not as many kicks.

Ty lost himself in the slow movements, his mind drifting easily as he turned, shifting his weight from one foot to the other.

The form itself addressed all four directions. When Ty found himself facing south suddenly, his hackles rose again. He continued the form, making himself turn away, run through every position.

However, now he knew that something was there. Funnily enough, his attention focused on the window just above his bed.

Ty tuned his senses, focusing on any hint of demon presence.

There. Just outside his window. A demon had passed through, though it had been sometime before. Seattle had been enjoying a warm fall. The rains hadn't come yet. So scents hung around for longer. He couldn't tell precisely how old the scent was, but it was at least a couple of weeks old. Maybe older.

What the hell? The demon wasn't still there, though it had deposited…something.

Ty took a shower, got dressed, made himself transform into his fully human form, before he braved the outdoors.

Bushes grew up under the window, something scratchy and currently leafless. Ty had a vague memory of it having flowers in the spring. He never paid any attention to that sort of thing.

It wasn't easy to get behind the bush. That was good to know, actually, that Ty's window wasn't easy to approach from the outside.

Ty scanned the ground, looking for whatever it was that the demon had dropped. It took him a moment to find the tiny rock that felt different than everything around it.

No, crystal. One of those corruption crystals. Christine had told him about them.

Why had the demons chosen him for one of their "presents"? And why hadn't Ty felt its influence until now?

Though, thinking back, Ty realized that he had been

more on edge, in general, when he'd been home. The corruption crystals worked slowly.

Surely not as slowly as that.

Ty reached out with a fully transformed claw to scoop the crystal up from the dirt.

As soon as he touched the thing, he couldn't help but growl.

Damn it! Those things were strong. And rattled the bars of the beast Ty held tightly caged inside of him.

His training and meditation had enabled him to resist for as long as he had.

He remembered Christine talking about how no one had been able to study or resist the crystals for more than a day or so.

Of course, she was talking about humans.

Ty had to find a damned container for this thing before it burned a hole in his hand, or caused his training to fail.

Who could he bring the corruption crystal to? Who could he tell about how he'd managed to avoid being influenced?

If only Nik was around! The shopkeeper might have known what to do with these things. Though he couldn't have told anyone if he had. He had to maintain his neutrality in order to stay alive in his small wooden body.

He'd given up that neutrality to help Christine win the last great battle. And had died in the process.

Maybe, though, there was something at his shop. Something that one of the human magicians could use.

Who owned the shop now? Ty didn't know. He was certain that Nik had left some sort of will. Was his shop for sale? Had anyone tried accessing the space since Nik had died?

Ty had some hunting to do. It wasn't going to be as fun as hunting a demon, no chasing or fighting. (Ty had to admit that he was something of an adrenaline junky.)

Still, he finally had something that could help Christine and the war effort, beyond his fruitless pursuit of Lars.

Humming, Ty put the crystal down and went back inside to see if he could find a container for the damned rock, then to call on Vern to see if he knew the status of Nik's shop.

CHAPTER SEVEN

"Sure, sure, I understand," Dennis said, nodding and sounding sympathetic while still trying to think how to get around this latest obstacle, to bring the *kith and kin* race of the Contigan into the fold, to lose their damned neutrality and actually chose a side.

His badass warrior princess sister had just handed the demons their *asses*, thank you very much. He would have thought that would have brought more of the *kith and kin* rallying to her side.

But noooooo. That wasn't good enough.

The beings who sat across the table—which still held the remains from their very excellent pastries and coffee— looked human enough. For lawyers. The pair of them wore power suits the same shade of shifty, smoke gray, with shirts bleached bright enough to make your eyes bleed. They had identical haircuts, almost military jarhead flattops, obviously expecting everyone to take their orders. Only their ties differentiated them, Luke in a blue power tie and Jack in a red one.

They looked enough alike to be brothers or cousins. Which as far as Dennis understood the race would be an accurate assessment. They weren't so much hatched as cloned.

Of course they'd choose to appear on the human plane as lawyers. They didn't have much physical ability when it came to fighting. In their native form, they appeared as tall will-o-the-wisp creatures, practically translucent and filled with light.

As magical fighters, they were practically unstoppable.

Dennis had been trying to recruit them for Christine's armies for many months. They'd always met with him, considered his proposals, then said no.

As they'd chosen the coffeeshop they always met at, Dennis didn't think it was the environment influencing them.

What could he say to get them to change their minds?

Dennis looked up to see them staring at him intently.

Uh, oh. Had he said that out loud?

Couldn't hurt at this point. "What could I tell you to get you to come to fight with us?" he said, not caring if he was repeating himself.

"We need a worthy foe," Jack finally answered. "These demons are hardly worth the effort."

Dennis had to work hard to not roll his eyes. Of course, the Contigan considered themselves all that. "Even an army of demons who were all fortified with the corruption crystals? I'd heard that they were quite a magical force to be reckoned with."

Interesting. Jack, and the other, Luke, glanced at each other, as if confirming their script. Before this, the two had seemed to always be so in sync with one another that Dennis had wondered if they'd written out their conversation ahead of time, then gamed it out a few times with different scenarios.

"But the demons you'll be facing now won't have the corruption crystals," Jack said. "They've given those up since losing the big battle to Princess Kizalynn."

"So they would have been a worthy foe before, but now they aren't?" Dennis said, aware that he was treading on thin ice, just this side of calling the Contigans cowards.

Jack considered his words before speaking. "There are some of the demons who might be worth battling. Those who are strong enough willed without artifice."

"Such as?" Dennis asked. He didn't know if Christine could arrange a battle with one branch of the demons just for the Contigan or not. Wouldn't hurt to ask.

He sometimes marveled at how much he'd changed since he'd started working for Christine fulltime. He hadn't considered himself a traditional type of guy. He'd quickly discovered that he was occasionally hesitant to operate without a net, that he needed to be more sure of himself and where he stood.

But as part of the new Dennis, he'd grown accustomed to listening more, to asking questions, to admitting ignorance.

Seemed he really was growing up.

Jack reeled off a long string of syllables that appeared to be a name.

How the hell was Dennis supposed to remember that?

His confusion must have shown, because Jack took pity on him. "The horse-headed demons who generally act as guards in hell. They are smarter than the average demon. Not as bribable. And they have greater magical abilities."

Dennis had no idea if Christine regularly fought those types of demons or not. "I'll need to check and see if we can arrange something," he said.

He was surprised at the predator smile he received, as if the sharks over there had just smelled blood in the water. "Do you have something in particular against these guys?" Dennis asked. "Something else I should tell the princess about?"

"A demonstration of her fighting techniques against such foes would go a long way toward assuring our mutual agreement when it comes to picking battles," Luke said.

It took Dennis a moment to translate. "Let me see what I can do," he said, standing up.

These two liked to shake hands, which always weirded Dennis out. Their skin was softer than any woman's he'd ever known, while a strength ran through the grip, like the flesh covered steel.

He sat back down after the pair of them had left, debating whether or not to get another cup of the excellent coffee they had here. He had a little time to kill before his next appointment, which fortunately was just down the street.

Two women came into the shop just as Dennis was getting ready to go. One looked vaguely familiar, with blonde-brown hair tied up in a ponytail, her skin sun-kissed. Her bright purple shirt stretched tightly across her really nice chest.

Dennis could swear he'd seen her before. But where?

When she looked over her shoulder, she gave him a smile and a nod.

She wasn't human. Or at least not fully human. No one was that perfect.

Still, Dennis couldn't remember where he'd first met her. It had to have been with Christine. The woman and her friend ordered their drinks and went to sit in the far corner, away from the front of the shop. It would be really awkward for him to go over there and introduce himself. Particularly since he didn't remember her name.

Wait. It started with an L. Louisa? Linda? Something.

His watch binged at him, reminding him of his next appointment before he had time to make up his mind.

Maybe the next time he saw her, he'd speak to her. He didn't have time that morning. And he'd have to remember to ask Christine about where he might have met such a beautiful woman before.

He caught her eye and nodded to her before he left the shop, not seeing the blinding smile she returned to him after he'd turned his back.

Through the rest of the day, though, he felt an inner glow that he didn't quite understand.

CHAPTER EIGHT

Ozlandia growled at two of the king's guard standing before her. They'd been found guilty of taking bribes. At least both of them had the grace to look abashed.

She stood taller than the pair of them, as she was uncommonly tall for a troll who had not a speck of royal blood in her. She was almost as tall as Princess Kizalynn. It was one of the reasons why they trained together, as the princess needed to regularly fight beings who were not just her height but taller.

"What do you have to say for yourselves?" Ozlandia asked finally.

They all stood in the tiny office Ozlandia used. It was barely big enough for three trolls. Six trolls wouldn't have been able to stand in a cluster in the center of the square stone floor without touching. No windows marred any of the solid rock walls—Ozlandia had joked that she could tunnel her way out if she was ever trapped there. Brightly burning oil lamps gave the room a golden glow. She had a tiny desk shoved into one corner, with a single chair behind it.

Broken weapons decorated all of the walls, weapons that had failed Ozlandia in one battle or another—axes, swords, pikes, as well as a couple of severely dented helmets. They were a constant reminder that she was one wrong step away from losing her life, an unlucky roll of the dice away from death. They made her train harder, as well as test herself.

She'd sworn that as she aged, if she ever felt her skills start to diminish, she would retire immediately.

Luckily, that time still appeared to be several decades from then.

The trolls standing in front of Ozlandia both shuffled from one foot to the other. They still wore the king's guard uniform, as did Ozlandia, consisting of a navy-blue vest with rings sewn into it, cropped brown wool pants, and black boots. They carried their silver peaked helmets under one arm, on the side where they hung their short stabbing swords. Both had the traditional bag full of sharp stones on the other side, and had axes strapped to their backs.

"We're sorry?" said Thrustikan, the one on the right and the younger of the two.

"I don't know what came over me," Franchila said, the words tumbling out. "I know it's wrong. I do," she emphasized.

Ozlandia couldn't help the chill that crept across her shoulders. She merely nodded though, encouraging the troll to continue.

"I shouldn't have done it. I know it's wrong. It's a stain

not just on my honor, but on my family's honor and the honor of the king's guard," Franchila continued.

The poor troll sounded contrite. Ozlandia didn't doubt that Franchila did know better. She'd been part of the guard for seven years. This was her first serious infraction. (No one really counted drinking a little too much and getting rowdy in a bar, which Franchila did on a semi-regular basis.)

The refrain of "I don't know what came over me" was growing horrifyingly familiar to Ozlandia.

The guard were being corrupted, influenced by unseen demon forces.

It wasn't easy to corrupt a troll. Demons had to work especially hard at it. They claimed it was because the trolls were so stupid. Ozlandia suspected it was because trolls were so tied to the earth. Good solid soil beneath their feet reminded them of their inherent strength.

"You're both on extended leave, starting now," Ozlandia said. "You need to take a few weeks away from the palace. Go back to your family farms. Play with your cousins and younger relations. Come back when you feel rested. And clean."

"But—but the war!" Franchila said. "You can't be sending us away!"

Ozlandia nodded, acknowledging the comment. "True. It will be difficult losing two more of the guard, particularly when we desperately need every able body we have to go to battle. However," Ozlandia paused, putting her words together carefully, "I need *able bodied* trolls. Trolls in full command of themselves. Not ones who sometimes act against the best interest of the rest of the guard. And the king."

She didn't want to come out and say that they'd been corrupted. Trolls rarely took that well. Besides, then they might go and attempt some "cure." Charlatans had sprung up, offering false purification rituals that merely relieved honest, hard-working trolls of their coin while not delivering a damned thing.

Playing with babies and younger, innocent trolls generally did the trick. Along with getting out of the palace, back to houses with solid soil floors instead of stone.

Ozlandia suspected that the palace, itself, was where most of the trolls she'd been sending home had been corrupted.

Franchila stood up straighter. "I understand, ma'am," she said, nodding curtly.

Thrustikan looked as though she might argue more, though she kept her piece at a sharp glance from Franchila.

"Come back and see me in three weeks," Ozlandia said. "Or when you feel fully in control of yourselves again. Not before. Leave all your gear here."

"Ma'am?" Franchila asked, looking puzzled.

"Civilian clothes for civilians," Ozlandia growled. "No armor. No uniform. No weapons. You hear me?"

They both hung their heads in shame.

Ozlandia cleared her throat.

"Yes, ma'am," they said in unison.

They'd be going home in disgrace, in plain clothes and not in their uniforms. Ozlandia couldn't help that.

However, all their gear would be gone over by the human magician who Christine had recommended, who would detect whether or not any of their gear had a demonic taint to it.

It was the second most likely cause for corruption. Ozlandia had no idea how so many good weapons had some sort of demonic influence coating them. Luckily, the blacksmith's guild had grown talented in melting down the old weapons and reshaping them, pure and clean.

"Dismissed," Ozlandia barked at the two guards. They both stood up straighter, saluted, and marched out of her office.

Ozlandia sighed and went over to her desk. Like most trolls, Ozlandia had an excellent memory. However, it was easier to keep track of the guard in large roll books.

It was a part of her commission as head of the king's guard that she'd gladly give up—having to record all the infractions for various guard members.

Each year, new roll books were created, each troll in the guard having a page dedicated to him or herself. The records from the previous years were magically copied over. Trolls who had died or retired were no longer in the books, and new trolls were added.

Because of the war, Ozlandia had had a new roll book created, one with every troll who had joined added to it.

First, Ozlandia added a large "C" to Franchila's page, marking that she'd been corrupted, followed by the annotation of the bribe. It wasn't fair to the troll to record the bribe first. Ozlandia was certain that the bribe had only occurred because Franchila had been corrupted. She did the same for Thrustikan, who was in the new roll book.

She spent a moment paging through the book of new members of the guard. A surprising number of them had all been corrupted, and recently—the existing guard was much more immune, it seemed.

There was something rotten here, in the heart of Trollville.

And Ozlandia had no idea how to combat it.

CHAPTER NINE

VERN STOOD ON THE SIDEWALK OUTSIDE OF WHAT appeared to be a derelict apartment building in the International District. Ty stood beside him. The morning was overcast, but Vern doubted that rain would be coming —the air was cool and crisp, not chewy and wet.

Cheap plywood boards covered the front windows, and graffiti and handbills covered the wood. The building itself had probably been grand at one point, though now the red brick was stained and blackened. The staircase leading up from the street was wide and made of marble that hadn't aged well. Wooden boards had also been attached on either side of a solid steel door, covering what had probably been leaded glass at one point.

"You sure this is the place?" Vern asked Ty, who kept his nose raised to the air, sniffing, like a coffee addict in search of his next hit. Ty wore a dirt-crusted blue-leather hat with a small brim in the front—the kind that train conductors used to wear. He was dressed in a casual heavy denim jacket, jeans, and solid boots.

Vern had found these wonderful, barefoot shoes that he now wore every time he had to go someplace and couldn't be barefoot. He also had on thick jeans, a blue and red Hawaiian shirt, and a bright yellow rain jacket.

"It was," Ty said, shrugging. "This used to be where the main portal to Nik's Trade Goods and Emporium stood. Can you sense anything?"

Vern shrugged. He reached across his chest and touched his fingers to his wand, sitting in an expressly made pocket where most guys would put their phones.

Huh. Vern would have sworn that he'd just seen… something. A flash of blue, perhaps.

Nik had left an extensive will. Christine had inherited three warehouses full of goods boxed up from estates that Nik had bought and had never gone through or catalogued. Other warehouses went to other beings, former customers of Nik's.

He had also left very specific instructions about the disposition of the shop. It was to remain empty and unused, the space magically powered and guaranteed for at least a decade, until "the right being came along." Nik had set up a trust to pay for the spells and the ingredients necessary.

If the right being hadn't come along in that time, the spells holding the space available would be stopped and the store would collapse in on itself.

What Ty and the others had guessed was that the "right being" meant someone who could open the portals to the shop. As far as Ty had been able to discern, though several beings had tried—humans, various *kith and kin*, as well as demons—no one had been able to get into the space yet.

Which was why Vern and Ty were now standing in front of what used to be the primary portal, so that Vern could give it a go.

Really, it was like that sword in the stone book that he'd had to read to both Dennis and Christine over and over again. The sword just waiting for the right hand to touch it.

Vern looked over at Ty, who shrugged. "May as well try it," he said. "Then we can go and get some coffee."

Vern couldn't help his grin. He *knew* that Ty had been looking for his next fix.

"All right," Vern said. He looked around. No one appeared to be paying any attention to them. An older Asian woman hurried by, not looking at the two foreigners staring at the decrepit old building.

Vern called up the power he held inside of himself, uncorking the effervescent stream. He didn't glow, not like Tina did when she was having a good day and fully felt the magic. He felt lighter, though, full of champagne bubbles and goodness.

He directed that flow around the pair of them, basically causing all who looked at them to immediately look away. There was just an order of magnitude between a distraction bubble and a shield, which meant that Vern could harden the magic around them to protect them in an instant.

Ty looked over at him. "Nice," he said.

Vern couldn't help but feel proud. He didn't need anyone's approval—that had been a problem for him his entire life, particularly when dealing with the corporate world and bosses. Still, it felt good that Ty, someone who Vern seriously respected, accepted his magic.

After another glance around, Vern pulled out his wand. He always felt better with it in his hand. It wasn't one of those kid's wands, made out of knobby wood. Instead, it was made from a blue resin, the kind used for really good fountain pens, with gold flecks floating in it. It didn't have an obvious head or tail, but he always knew which end to hold.

There wasn't that much magic in the wand itself, which had surprised Vern. Instead, it was a focusing device, a way for Vern to send a beam of power instead of a widespread wave.

"Here goes nothing," Vern muttered to himself.

With the wand in one hand, Vern brought up his other, and with both hands, outlined the shape of a door, flat across the top, then down square on either side.

Nothing happened. No portal sprang up.

"That's what I figured—" Vern started to say, turning to Ty, who was staring hard at the opening.

"Did you see that?" Ty interrupted.

"See what?" Vern asked, turning back to the doorway.

"I thought I saw a flash of blue. Just for a moment," Ty said slowly.

"I thought I saw that when we first came up," Vern admitted. "Figured I was just seeing things."

"No, you probably saw it too, then," Ty said. "The flash of a portal doorway. Don't know if it's just there, a remnant from before, or if that means something."

"Should I try again?" Vern asked.

"Yeah," Ty said, nodding, all of his attention still focused on the doorway.

Vern sketched the outline of a square door again.

This time, he thought he saw the same blue flash that he'd seen before.

"We're close," Ty said after a moment. He nodded and turned to Vern. "Thought I even smelled a hint of wood and magic for a second."

"So what am I doing wrong?" Vern asked. "Or do you want to try it?"

Ty snorted. "Already tried," he admitted. "Most of the afternoon, yesterday, after I found out what the will said. Didn't even get this far."

"You should try again," Vern said.

Ty nodded, bringing his own hands up and sketching a door.

No hint of blue this time.

"Describe the old portal to me," Vern told Ty.

The demon hunter shrugged. "Nik used to have a partner, Joey, who would work the night markets and bring in tourists. Joey would be the one who activated the portal for out-of-towners. Once a customer had been in the shop once, they could find the portal themselves."

"Where is this Joey now?" Vern asked.

"Retired," Ty said. "The lawyers got in contact with him as per Nik's will. Nik had left him a nice chunk of cash for helping him out for all those years."

"Has Joey tried opening the portal?" Vern asked.

Ty shrugged. "Don't know. Don't think he wants the store."

Vern nodded. "What else can you tell me about the portal? Was it just there, at the top of the stairs?"

"Yup," Ty said. He paused for a moment, thinking. "To a non-magical being, it just appeared as though the door to the apartment building had opened. To a magical being, the portal showed up as an oval of blue light."

Vern and Ty turned toward each other, both of them having the exact same thought.

"Have we been going about this all wrong?" Vern asked. "Sketching a square doorway instead of an oval?"

Ty nodded slowly. "Could be. That's how all other portals are created. Even the ones going into the store. It was only the first time, through the first portal, that you went through an oval."

"Let's try it," Vern said, turning toward the empty doorway again.

Instead of using both hands to sketch a square opening, Vern used just his wand and drew a big oval.

A faint blue shimmer of light appeared.

Vern sketched the oval a second, then a third time, before the light solidified, glowing brightly, with a solid black interior.

"You got it!" Ty exclaimed excitedly.

Vern nodded, though he didn't feel as jubilant as he'd expected.

Sure, he'd opened up the portal to Nik's store.

Just what would they find inside?

CHAPTER TEN

CHRISTINE DIDN'T LIKE HOW CRESTFALLEN KING Garethen looked when she'd told him that they needed to talk.

She really didn't care for the way his eyes suddenly grew shifty. He appeared to shrink, his red sleeveless tunic suddenly hanging on him, no longer tight across his muscular chest, his crown seemingly heavier, weighing down his long white hair.

"I see," King Garethen said as his face lost all expression. He walked around and sat behind his desk instead of taking the seat beside Christine.

She tried not to assume that was a bad sign, Garethen putting that great hulking stone desk between them. Still, she had serious things to say, things that the king needed to hear, not just her uncle.

Christine had tried preparing a speech, figuring out what she'd say. However, that had never been her way. In the end, she just winged it.

"I saw what you promised the cambions," she said

after a moment. She tried to keep her tone less confrontational than she felt.

"Ah, did you now?" the king said, leaning back in his chair, away from the desk and away from her. "It was perfectly within my right to do so," he added, sounding defensive.

Christine nodded. "And I saw why you did it. You thought that you were doing the right thing, trying to help out beings who were being persecuted by the demons."

"Exactly!" the king said, looking relieved. "I had to do it."

"The problem is, they're demons," Christine said. "You should have known that they'd never stick to the original bargain."

"That's not my fault," King Garethen said. "I can't be held to blame for that."

Christine held onto her temper, at least for the moment. "Don't you want to know what they're doing?" Huh. She really managed to keep her voice mild. It was going to be much harder to do that later on, she was certain.

"Ah, sure," the king said, looking confused.

"They're carrying other demons, bad demons, utterly corrupt demons, across the bridge. On their backs," Christine said. "The other demons wouldn't be able to cross the bridge on their own. Because you opened up a loophole, *all* the worlds of the *kith and kin* are now at risk. It's how the demons have been able to attack so many places that they shouldn't have been able to have access to."

The king looked shocked. Then he shook his head. "No. It's in the contract. Just cambions can cross the bridge."

"You never specified what they could or couldn't carry with them," Christine pointed out.

The king just shook his head. "How could I know?"

Clearly, he was not going to accept any responsibility for what he'd done.

"What did you get in exchange?" Christine asked. That had been the thing that she hadn't been able to determine. What had the demons offered the king in exchange for access?

"Gold," the king said. He sounded defensive. "We needed the money for the war effort, that *you* were leading," he reminded her. "I'm not made of money, you know. I needed more coins for weapons, armor, paying soldiers, all like that."

"How much gold?" Christine asked. She knew that the king would lie about whatever he'd been given. Still, she wanted a starting estimate.

The gold itself had probably been corrupted. Christine had seen the same thing with Tina. The thing her human sister held most dear had been her wand. She wouldn't give it up, even after they'd managed to get rid of all the other things corrupting her.

The king must have a greedy side to him that Christine hadn't happened upon before.

"Why?" the king asked, sounding suspicious now. "Why do you need to know?"

Christine sat very still. This was truly the heart of the corruption. There were probably other items in the royal treasury, or the hall of viewing, that held corrupted artifacts, gifts with corruption crystals embedded in them that had slowly worn away at the inner goodness of the trolls and the court.

Then again, her uncle and the court had been corrupted before by Chamberlain McDommokin. She'd always suspected that the chamberlain himself had been infected by demons, though she'd never had the chance to prove it, as the man had hung himself while being held for trial. Demonic corruption would explain the metallic colors he wore—the gold and silver—instead of the bright gem colors that were more natural to trolls.

"I need to know, uncle," Christine said gently after a few moments, "because you're going to have to give up all of it."

"No," the king said immediately. "I will not have it taken from me. You don't need it."

"It's corrupted," Christine pointed out. "It needs to be cleansed. Purified."

"Good. I'll just perform a cleansing spell," the king said.

Christine knew that wouldn't be enough. And she wasn't about to lie to the king. "Even after all the demonic taint has been removed, you can't keep the gold. It will just continue to worm its way into your heart. Have you spent any of it? On the war?"

"I have," the king said proudly.

"And do you regret it to this day?" Christine challenged.

"Of course I do! It was *my* gold," King Garethen said.

"Even though it kept my soldiers—your people—

alive? Helped stop the demons from winning the Great War?"

The king appeared to have no answer to that.

"You must let go of the gold," Christine said. "All of it."

She knew it was hopeless. The king would never give it all up. Like Tina, he'd hide away part of it. "And the palace must be cleansed. There's corruption here. I can feel it." She hadn't thought about it before she'd arrived that afternoon, but now she could practically smell it.

"And if I don't?" King Garethen said belligerently.

"You must," Christine said, finding herself growing angry again, though she knew it wasn't really Garethen's fault. "The corruption is spreading. It's starting to affect the troops."

"You just need to recruit better," the king said. "Stop killing so many of them."

"I what?" Christine said, starting to lose her temper. "The king's guard and all the other trolls who fight with me are the best in all the worlds. They have fought and died to protect not just Trollville but the human world and the planes of the *kith and kin* from the demons. I will not have their memory or their honor corrupted by a demon lover."

Oops. That was probably going too far.

"I am *not* a demon lover," the king growled at her. "And why are we protecting all these places outside of Trollville? Shouldn't we be more focused on just our own plane?"

"What, like the humans?" Christine sneered. "They've been trying to start a 'humans first' campaign." Vern and the others had managed to get enough of the humans to vote for the magic council to continue to support the war effort, but it had been close.

"A troll first campaign does have a nice ring to it," King Garethen said, leaning forward across his desk. "Yes. Maybe we need to pull more trolls back, to protect here, instead of sending our troops out across the planes."

"But that's just what the demons want!" Christine said, shocked. "If we pull back, particularly now, the demons will win the Great War."

"I don't care," the king said stubbornly. "I am your king. And I am ordering at least half the troops home."

"And if I don't obey?" Christine asked, her voice quiet, her anger going from burning hot to white cold.

"Then I will disinherit you," the king said simply. "You will no longer be my heir."

"I don't want your throne," Christine said, her rage building. "I'm trying to stop the demons from winning."

"Really?" the king said.

Christine didn't like the way his tone had turned oily.

"Because as far as I know, the only way for me to withdraw my promise to the cambions is for me to either be killed or to abdicate my throne."

Christine sat with her lips pressed tightly together. He was right.

"So while you can talk all you want about demonic influence, I see what you're really after. Nothing will satisfy you other than this crown." The king rose up, standing, his anger buffeting Christine.

"I will not have you disrespecting me, dishonoring

your king, accusing me of cooperating with the demons," Garethen yelled.

"But that's exactly what you've been doing!" Christine said, standing herself. "You've been cooperating with the cambion. You've let them into all the worlds! And you've taken their gold!"

They stared at each other, tense, angry. Christine saw again just how heavy the king's crown looked that afternoon, how beady his eyes had grown.

He was starting to look like a demon himself.

"Keep the damned gold," Christine snapped. "I don't care if you hoard it for the rest of your days. Just let me at least clean the damned palace."

She couldn't depose the king. Not while she had a war to win.

Afterward, though…

"I suppose you're be bringing in human magicians," the king sneered.

Christine blinked, stung. "What's wrong with humans?" she asked. "Humans saved my life."

It had always been in insult in trollish to be called a *human lover*.

"I don't want humans here," King Garethen said, his anger still apparent.

"I will bring in someone else," Christine said. She knew she had to compromise on this topic if she was to get anywhere at all.

Ty could locate everything that had been tainted. And he was only partially human. She'd just have to find one of the *kith and kin* who could work with him to dispose of the tainted goods.

"Fine," the king said. "You can cleanse the palace, though you won't find much."

Christine kept her snort of derision to herself. She doubted that very much.

"And you need to send half my troops home," he added.

"But—"

"You heard me," the king growled. "Half the king's guard."

Christine hated how she automatically found a way to weasel around his command. "I will send home half the king's guard," she said slowly. "But I get to clean *all* the public areas of the palace and its grounds."

"Fine," the king said.

Christine gave the king a curt nod, then turned to leave. Before she got to the door, she looked back over her shoulder. "Someday, uncle, I hope that you will be able to give up your gold voluntarily."

"Or else?" the king challenged.

Christine shook her head. "Not an 'or else.' Not a threat. Merely a warning. Before it completely corrupts you."

She quickly left the room before she would say more words that she'd come to regret.

CHAPTER ELEVEN

AFTER MUCH DEBATE WITH HIMSELF, LARS PUT OFF pouring his demons into the planes of the rowdy boys one more week. He had to get some of his other plans into order first.

He'd had a lovely breakfast of steaming entrails, fresh from the body of an innocent. (Lars never probed too carefully about the race of such a victim, firmly believing in the adage that you never actually wanted to see how the sausage got made.) Plus coffee, burned and dark enough to stand a spoon in.

He sat behind the desk in his command center, or so he'd taken to calling his childhood room, now that he had everything arranged to his liking. His huge, industrial desk dominated the space. He'd placed a couple of deliberately uncomfortable chairs on the other side, just to remind any demon who came to visit who was actually in charge. Maps of the various worlds of the *kith and kin* still decorated the walls, covered in glorious red to indicate his victories.

The only thing missing from his office was Christine's head. The place of honor still rested immediately behind him, mockingly him with its emptiness.

A sharp knock brought Lars back to the present. He took another sip of his dark brew before calling, "Come in!"

One of his minions opened the door and let in a tall, broad-shouldered young human-looking male. He wore a plain gray T-shirt over a well-muscled chest, jeans, and plain sneakers. His blond-brown hair had been buzzed short, giving him a military look. He had dark brown eyes that glanced around the room suspiciously.

"You wanted to see me?" he growled, standing and facing Lars.

"Please, Joe, sit," Lars said, indicating the chairs on the other side of the desk.

"What do you want?" Joe said, still standing.

"So you haven't forgiven me for getting you into trouble?" Lars asked.

The young being in front of him suddenly grew a formidable set of troll tusks, his skin turning a dark green-brown. "I was the one who fucked up, not you," Joe said. "And not by listening to you. For not finishing the job."

"Really?" Lars said. While he'd gamed out this particular scenario, he hadn't given it much more than a ten-percent chance that this was the way that Joe would feel. "What do you mean?"

"I destroyed the fairy bridge, as you asked me to," Joe said, nodding. "That was the right thing to do," he added defensively. "Anyone with eyes could see that Christine had built it wrong."

"Go on," Lars said, encouraging the young troll.

"But then, I should have gone back to Trollville," Joe said. "Immediately. Gotten the hell out of the human plane for good."

"The bridge was broken at the time," Lars couldn't help but point out.

Joe shrugged. "There are other ways. But I should have gone home. Let my family know what was going on. How Christine and the royals were going to ruin everything. Again."

"Have you been home?" Lars couldn't help but ask.

Joe shook his head. "Nope. Not intending to, either. Going to let Trollville burn. That's the only way for it to be rebuilt as it should be."

"I see," Lars said. This was an interesting scenario, one that he actually hadn't planned on. He didn't think he'd find a troll who was so willing to tear it all down.

Particularly not one who he'd bribed and corrupted so easily before.

"Seriously, a *human* could do a better job of ruling right now," Joe said, exasperated.

"Why don't you tell me all about it?" Lars said, indicating the chairs in front of his desk.

"Why bother? There isn't anything I can do about it," Joe said.

"But there might be something I can do about it," Lars suggested quietly.

"Oh yeah? Like what?" Joe said, finally throwing himself into a chair.

Lars could tell that Joe regretted it instantly, but that was all right. Lars wanted Joe prickly and on his guard.

That way, he could tell himself that he wasn't being influenced by a demon. Because that sort of seduction is supposed to feel good, right? Comfortable, even?

"I know that you had to bear the brunt of your actions. You had your wages garnished by the Host, for destroying the fairy bridge," Lars said. "Trust me, if I'd learned about it earlier, I would have done something about it. But I was put into jail for five years. Not much I could have done," Lars lied.

Joe merely grunted.

"But now that I'm out, let's set things right. I'll pay off the rest of your bond," Lars said.

Joe's eyes grew comically huge.

"And I'll send you back to Trollville with a large chest of gold, just as a way of showing my gratitude," Lars continued.

"What's the catch?" Joe asked.

Lars wanted to cheer. Yet another indication that Joe had no clue that Lars was sinking hooks back into his soul.

"I want you to go back to the court and talk about your experiences. Particularly with Christine. There are those who would listen, many more than there used to be. Trolls who are unhappy with the current king," Lars assured him.

"They'll just decide on another from the Te'Dur line," Joe said, disgusted. "My family doesn't have a chance."

"Why is that?" Lars asked. "You're fine, upstanding trolls whose heritage, as I understand these things, goes back just as far as the current monarchy."

"But we don't have magic!" Joe said hotly. "Royal trolls

are supposed to have magic. My family's power is spotty, at best."

"Do you honestly think magic is what gives the current regime its power?" Lars asked. "Or is it the key to their downfall?"

Joe looked interested. "Tell me more," he said.

———

IT DIDN'T TAKE LONG FOR LARS TO GET JOE TO AGREE to go back to Trollville with a large sum of gold and a mission: to remind the court of other, *legitimate* heirs that the king might be able to select.

Lars didn't expect Joe to succeed in getting himself assigned as an heir. His family wasn't well enough connected to the current royal family, and they did have a spotty record when it came to magical power.

However, wouldn't it be a coup for Lars if he got the old king unseated, and the new one had no magical defenses against demonic influence?

CHAPTER TWELVE

"Ow."

Ty found himself on his ass at the bottom of the stairs. He'd tried going through the portal to Nik's old shop ahead of Vern, seeing as he was the stronger of the pair of them. If anything was waiting for them on the other side, it would have to go through Ty first before reaching Vern.

The shop, and the portal, appeared to have a different idea.

"Are you okay?" Vern asked, standing at the top of the stairs and looking down to where Ty had flown after being bounced so hard by the portal.

"Yeah," Ty said, pushing himself back up to standing. He wasn't getting too old for this kind of shit. Really. He had a lot of good years left.

Somedays, though, his body let him know that he was no longer a teenager, but in his thirties. He also never seemed to have fully recovered from being so thoroughly poisoned by that demon.

"Seems as though since I opened the portal, I need to

go through first," Vern said, having come to the same conclusion as Ty.

"I'll be right behind you," Ty assured him, though he knew that might not be the truth. Portals were funny that way, and though beings went through together, they got separated and arrived minutes apart.

"All right," Vern said. He raised up his wand, holding it at the ready, then disappeared into the glowing blue oval.

Ty went through the opening moments later.

When he stepped into the other side, he realized that he'd been held in limbo for a few minutes before he'd arrived in Nik's shop.

Vern stood on the other side of the room, next to the counter at the front of the store. Dim light shone down from the ceiling, like bright sunlight filtered through the canvas of a tent.

"Don't!" Ty shouted as he saw Vern's hand lift toward his mouth and put something in it.

Too late.

"What the hell was that?" Ty asked. He grabbed Vern's hand before he reached for the second bright blue glowing nodule sitting on the front counter.

Vern shook his head as if coming out of a spell. He pointed with his other hand at the paper the nodule had been sitting on.

The words "Eat Me" had been written there with a black marker.

"I couldn't stop myself," Vern said. He sounded worried. "But I don't feel bad. Or off," he said after a moment. "I want to read what's on the other paper."

Ty nodded and let go of the human's hand. What kind of trap had Nik set for whoever could open the portal to his shop? Or had it been someone other than Nik?

Vern slid the nodule off the paper onto the glass counter and picked up the note. Ty could see that it had been written in Nik's flowing hand.

Vern started to read out loud.

"Welcome! You've discovered the portal to what used to be called Nikolai's Trade Goods and Emporium. What you just swallowed was an enchanted protection spell, guaranteed to ward off any and all magical influence. While the spell is still working, no one will be able to suggest a price or a deal and make you agree to it."

"Huh," Ty replied. "That spell would have sure been useful to know earlier." He was going to have to make sure that the magical council knew about it.

Vern nodded and went back to reading.

"I made two. They're quite expensive and take a good deal of practice and knowledge to create. The first should last about a year's time. You should use the second as a template, so that you can create your own. When the first starts to wear off, you'll feel compelled to swallow the second. This gives you two years to operate free of unwanted influence. Hopefully by that time you'll have been able to create your own and so can continue to operate the shop."

Ty gave a low whistle. Christine had told him what had happened to Nik, how he'd moved his consciousness from his human body into the wooden one so that he would never be influenced by demons again.

"The books on the counter list inventory and suppliers, at least those who existed when I closed the shop. While this is a good place to start, you'll also need to develop your own networks."

A tall stack of leather-bound journals sat on the side of the counter. Vern touched one with reverence.

"Good luck! And remember to treat all beings fairly."
Nikolai

Vern set the letter down on the counter and slid over one of the books, opening it before Ty could say anything else. He nodded to himself while Ty looked around the rest of the shop.

It seemed much larger than Ty had remembered it. Empty wooden shelf units marked off ten rows. The walls no longer held posters advertising various products. Ty smelled dust, as if the shop had sat empty for much longer than just a few weeks.

Movement caught his eye. He watched Vern reach out with his wand and absent mindedly tap it on the edge of the counter while all his attention was still absorbed by the book he held.

Blue light briefly flashed across the edge of the counter, outlining the top of it. Then the light spread, flowing up the wall behind the counter, up to the ceiling.

The overhead lights suddenly came on full strength. They looked like human florescent lights, metal cases holding long glowing tubes. Ty knew that no electricity came into the shop—it was powered by magic.

Seemed as though the shop had chosen Vern, as he now had the ability to run the place.

"I'll just see myself out," Ty said after a few moments.

Vern nodded and turned another page, seemingly fascinated by the lists of magical ingredients, suppliers, wholesale and retail prices.

Ty looked around the shop again. It wouldn't be the same with Vern running it. First of all, it was likely to be much more colorful. Vern had unzipped his bright yellow jacket and exposed the blue and red Hawaiian shirt he wore. The walls would reflect his choices, Ty suspected. Possibly the lights as well.

It was easy enough for Ty to form a portal to take him back to the street. He knew that Vern would be safe, that no one else would be able to enter the store unless Vern allowed it.

Ty turned up his jacket collar against the cold. There had to be some good coffee down here someplace. Then he'd go visit Kanishka, the head of the magical council, let her know the news about Vern, as well explain how Ty himself appeared to be able to withstand the corruption crystals.

CHAPTER THIRTEEN

Tina tried not to sigh like an overly dramatic teenager, though that was *exactly* how she felt that morning. Plus, she didn't want Malcom, her old magic teacher, to feel pity for her or something equally obnoxious.

They sat in a coffeeshop up in the Queen Anne neighborhood, not too far from Malcom's house. The shop actually sold more tea than coffee, but Tina could be magnanimous—even those weirdos needed someplace to go for their fix. A group of mothers sat around the table at the back, each with a huge, ostentatious stroller parked beside them. Tina tried to ignore them, but the catty tone of their conversation kept setting her back up.

The shop itself had lovely, warm, orange-colored walls, with dark brown shelves holding tins of tea. Windows along two walls let in what little light there was given the cloudy day. It felt cheery and comfortable in a way that Tina sincerely appreciated.

"I just—I don't know how to balance what's inside

me," Tina admitted. She hadn't bothered telling her adoptive parents about her struggles. They just would have looked worried then sent her to yet another shrink. Honestly, they just didn't get it and never would.

However, Tina knew that keeping her struggles just to herself was a sure path to failure. Someone needed to know about the darkness inside her that she could never completely banish. Or else the dark thoughts might take over again.

Tina did *not* want to go back down that path.

She'd chosen Malcom, her original magic teacher, the one who'd also taught Vern and unleashed his full potential. Malcom was calmness itself. She'd never known anyone who was so grounded, yet at the same time, open and friendly. She'd always thought of him as the African-American version of Mr. Rogers.

He even dressed that way sometimes. Today he wore an argyle sweater vest, the pattern of diamonds across the chest done in various shades of blue. Under that was a blue shirt that looked soft.

Malcom was so comfortable in his own skin. Could he teach her that trick?

"I'm not sure what you're asking me about," Malcom admitted, his dark hands wrapped around the white coffee mug. "Your powers are darker than they used to be, I can see that."

"Yes," Tina said, nodding. "But I don't know how to use just a bit of that darkness. How to blend it and not let it take over. How to not let that dark power overwhelm the bright light."

"You know that having a bit of darkness mixed in with

the light is normal, right?" Malcom said. "Everyone has that."

Tina blinked, surprised. "I've never really felt the darker side of my power before," she said.

"Trust me, everyone's got both," Malcom said. "We all have urges and feel the need for petty revenge. Or even earth-shattering deaths."

"But how to balance them?" Tina asked. "I can't just ignore them. I've tried that. When I do that, the darkness comes trickling in." She lowered her voice, as well as stared fixedly at the mug in front of her. "It scares me," she admitted quietly.

The hiss of the espresso machine at the counter seemed to be giving unwanted commentary, an expression of displeasure at her weakness.

"It's not easy to find the balance," Malcom said after a moment. "And everyone's mix is going to be different."

"That's not helpful," Tina said. She tried to keep the growl out of her voice. Huh. Maybe she'd been spending too much time with Christine. She did feel a lot more growly lately.

The coffee klatch in the back of the shop appeared to be breaking up. The mothers steered their massive strollers past the table where Malcom and Tina sat. A couple accidently bumped into Malcom's chair as they went by.

Not all of them apologized for doing so.

Malcom waited until they'd all passed before he spoke again. "That sort of thing. Bumping into the only black man they're likely to meet for the week," he said, nodding at the door where a few of the mothers had gathered outside, still chatting. "Could be innocent. Could be deliberate."

Tina nodded. She'd thought the same.

"Could I get angry at them? Absolutely. Maybe send a curse their way, a wave of bad luck to follow them for the day? Like the tires on their minivans suddenly punctured, their hair driers going on the fritz, or even the microwave no longer working?" Malcom gave her a wide grin. "Sure. I could do all those things. Would it do any good?"

It surprised Tina that Malcom appeared to actually be asking her, that it wasn't a rhetorical question.

"It would make you feel better. Wouldn't it?" she asked, still searching for that balance.

"No, it wouldn't," Malcom said.

Tina raised her eyebrows at him. "Not at all?"

"Okay, so maybe a little. But that's a momentary spike of gleeful spite. In the long run, it wouldn't be worth it. There's an old saying about how whatever you put out into the world will be returned threefold." Malcom stopped and sipped at his coffee. "Even if that bad luck didn't come back to haunt me, I wouldn't have made the world a better place."

"Momentary satisfaction versus long term happiness?" Tina said, still trying to put the pieces together.

"Exactly," Malcom said.

Tina shook her head. She felt like giving that exasperated sigh again. "That's all well and good in theory. How do I put it into practice?"

"You don't give in," Malcom told her solemnly. "Every day. There are demons who are worth fighting. Save your energy for those. You have to keep turning away from the darkness in the meanwhile. Making better choices."

"That sounds like a lot of work," Tina said. "Like a constant struggle."

"There isn't a one-time cure for this sort of ailment," Malcom said. "It's a daily, hourly thing. You'll just have to make the right choice. Every time. It will grow easier," he said.

"So that's the key? Don't let it overwhelm me? Just ignore it?" Tina said. She tried not to sound as frustrated as she felt.

"No. You have to acknowledge that you have a choice," Malcom said. "Then make the right choice. Every time."

"But what if I fail? Or mess up?" Tina asked.

"You forgive yourself," Malcom said. "Easier said than done, I know. And you make a better choice the next time."

Tina sat for a moment, feeling both sides welling up inside her, the dark as well as the light. "I don't know if that will be enough," she said after a moment. "I might need more help. It's too…tempting."

Malcom nodded. "All right. Let me make some inquiries. Let's see if I can get you something to help, particularly at the start of this."

"Thank you," Tina said. Though people who practiced magic didn't necessarily casually touch each other, or anyone actually, she still reached across the table and briefly squeezed Malcom's hand. "What you said will help some of the time. But what's inside me is bigger than that."

"Then we've moved beyond my pay grade," Malcom assured her. "I won't mention your name, but I have an idea of who might be able to help. Let me check, first."

"Thank you," Tina said again.

Maybe, maybe there was hope for her after all.

CHAPTER FOURTEEN

King Garethen grumbled as he hurried past the hall of viewing. That damned Thothian was still there, working with one of the king's own blacksmiths.

Garethen had thought that by refusing Kizalynn's first offer of a magician to detect supposed demon influence that he'd stymie her for a longer period of time, and therefore he'd be able to sneak more of the gifts out of the hall of viewing.

He'd easily been able to reject her first suggestion of Ty Brooks, demon hunter. The creature was part human, and Garethen had specifically told her no humans.

But she'd come prepared with a second set of names of beings who could work together. So he hadn't had any time. Plus, once he grudgingly approved, she called them up and set them to work immediately.

The Thothian—Peter was his name—wasn't much better than the damned demon hunter, but Garethen couldn't find anything to reject him. He had the head of a bird, with a long beak and rows of black feathers for hair, on top of a mostly human body.

He'd thought the Thothians were merely scribes, only concerned with their one hundred plus volumes of unreadable poetry. However, it turned out they were also powerful magicians.

Damn it! Those were *his* gifts. Sent to the court to honor *him*. He should have marked those as off limits to Kizalynn. But she'd specified all public places in the palace, and you didn't get much more public than the hall of viewing.

The hall had been set up specifically for the best of the gifts that the king received. Merchants who were lucky enough to have their goods displayed there told all their customers about it. It was good for business.

Admittedly, most of the gifts the king received were immediately re-gifted to ungrateful relatives, greedy courtiers, or even worse, as bribes for other *kith and kin* kingdoms.

Still. They were *his* gifts. Things that had been given to *him*. He should have known that Kizalynn would insist on using the damned Thothian to detect demonic influence there.

Next, she'd probably want to inspect the court room, just to get rid of his throne.

There had to be a way to stop her before she robbed him blind.

Garethen continued onto his study. At least she hadn't stooped to "inspecting" that room. Possibly he could claim that it was private, but he doubted she would listen to him. It seemed to her that only bedchambers were private, and everything else was fair game.

However, the king's study no longer soothed his heart as it once did. True, the huge purple geode on the far wall did look splendid. His desk, carved out of solid granite, held a certain gravitas for him. Narrow slits took up the far wall, allowing only a small amount of outdoor light into his sanctuary.

He didn't understand what bothered him about the place, though. Was it the fight he'd had with Kizalynn? Or something else? His secret closet where he hid his chests of gold was the most comfortable place in the palace anymore. He didn't want to admit that he'd taken to sleeping there, feeling the safest in that spot.

Why wasn't his study as comfortable anymore? It seemed to be missing something.

It wasn't because this place was clear of demonic influence, at least according to Kizalynn, was it? No, that was just foolishness.

The king didn't have long to fidget behind his desk before his first appointment of the afternoon arrived. The king was meeting with a young troll who'd spent much time in the human world. Seemed he'd met Kizalynn there.

Garethen hadn't been inclined to agree to meeting this Josekanly Zelelinna D'Angelino, even though his family had been part of the court forever.

Josekanly had been very free with his gold, though, in order to get himself an appointment.

The king figured he may as well hear what the young troll had to say.

And there he was. He had the broad shoulders of youth, and muscular arms that proclaimed he'd been in many battles. His skin was a shade too brown for Garethen's taste—most of the troll royalty had more of a green tinge to their skin. Proud tusks shot up from his lower jaw, surprisingly unscarred. Maybe he'd just been lucky in battle.

He wore a dark brown sleeveless vest, finely made, with a pattern of broad flowers stitched in white thread across the chest. His pants were a darker brown, and he wore common straw sandals that Garethen secretly envied —he knew just how comfortable those shoes were.

Around his neck he wore a thick gold chain. It didn't look like jewelry, but like an actual heavy chain. How much was that worth?

Josekanly stopped just inside the door and gave the king a deep bow. "My lordship. It's an honor to be allowed to speak with you today."

King Garethen felt mildly reassured. Maybe it had been the right thing to speak with this troll, in private and not in front of the entire court.

"Please, please, come in," the king said, rising and gesturing to the chairs on the other side of the desk, before sitting again himself. "How is your mother, the lovely Lady Zelelinna?" He had taken the time to ask about Josekanly's family before meeting with him. His mother had married beneath her, at least according to the keeper of the records. D'Angelino wasn't a farmer, but he didn't attend the court.

It was probably why poor Josekanly had no magic whatsoever.

"My mother is doing well. Thank you for asking," Josekanly said. His smile seemed slightly strained.

The king knew better than to ask after his father, who had been killed during a battle when Josekanly had been just a boy.

"She sends her greetings and promises to come pay a visit to the court as soon as she is able," Josekanly continued on. The words sounded rote, as if he'd said them a lot recently.

"Is she ill?" Garethen asked out of politeness.

"She truly loved my father, and has never fully recovered since his untimely demise," Josekanly said. "She will come to the court and pay her respects as soon as she feels able to."

Again, words that had a rote feeling to them.

"How have you enjoyed your time here in the court?" Garethen said. "You've never been here before, have you?"

Josekanly shook his head. "No, sire. It's been such an honor. I cannot thank you enough for having extended this courtesy to me."

"You're welcome," the king said. What did this young troll want? Why was he buttering up the king?

"I had the pleasure of meeting Christine on the human plane," Josekanly said.

"Kizalynn," the king absently corrected him. "She's Princess Kizalynn."

"Right," Josekanly said, nodding. "That's right. But I met her when she was just Christine, before she'd discovered her heritage, and I was merely Joe. I believe I was the first troll she'd ever met."

"Interesting," King Garethen said. Of course, he

should have known that Kizalynn would set her spy on him. Though this Josekanly wasn't a very good spy if the first thing he did was admit to being a friend of Kizalynn's.

"She was struggling on the human plane," Josekanly said leaning closer. "I tried to help her the best I could, to show her what it meant to be a real troll, but…" He shrugged and leaned back.

King Garethen found himself nodding in agreement. "But she'd been so influenced by that damned changeling spell! Too human. Far too human."

He regretted the words as soon as he'd spoken them. Kizalynn had actually turned into a really neat troll, someone whose company he enjoyed.

Well, until recently, when she'd decided to force him from the throne.

Josekanly nodded in agreement, though. "She was so wrapped up in her magic. I tried to stop her, you know, from destroying the fairy bridge the first time."

"Really?" the king asked, surprised. "Tell me about it." Kizalynn had never really talked much about it.

Josekanly laid out the story, about how her air element had been tied to that bridge. But she, so very selfishly, wouldn't take the time to figure out how to just draw the element out.

"If she's so damned magical, shouldn't she have been able to do that? To just draw out her element? Instead of having to wreck the bridge?" Josekanly growled.

"Yes. You're right. I hadn't thought of that," the king said. He was really starting to take a shine to this young troll.

"So then, she started to rebuild it. That first bridge

she'd built? It would have put all trolls to shame. We know how to construct good solid bridges. As well as buildings and other things. Like this fine desk of yours, or the palace. That first attempt of hers would have fallen over during the first storm." He shook his head with disgust. "I was *saving* her future embarrassment by pulling it down."

"Thank you for that," King Garethen said. "I know you'll never hear any gratitude from her."

Josekanly shrugged. "It was my pleasure. But more importantly, it was my duty. I know what duty and honor and family means."

Finally! Someone who understood.

"Did you see what she's doing here?" the king asked. "Going through the palace and 'cleansing' it. I think we both know what that actually means."

"Such greed," Josekanly said, shaking his head. "It doesn't suit her."

"No, no it doesn't," the king agreed.

"Now, this may be a delicate subject," Josekanly said, leaning forward in his chair again. "And I may be speaking out of turn. However, in my family I've observed that those with the most, want even more."

"What do you mean?" King Garethen said, suddenly suspicious. Those words sounded like an accusation against his own wealth.

"Those trolls who don't work in the good earth for a living. Those who use magic for even the most everyday tasks. They're never satisfied with what they have," Josekanly said. "You, for instance."

Garethen couldn't contain his growl. "What about me?"

"No, no, you misunderstand me," Josekanly said, instantly placating the king. "Rumor has it that you disguise yourself and go to town on your own. That you regularly mingle with the common people and those who aren't of the court. Am I right?"

The king shrugged, not willing to confirm or deny.

"While Christine—Kizalynn—she relies on magic for *everything*. She keeps herself isolated that way. Instead of having servants or regularly mingling with trolls or other beings who don't have magic. It isn't good for her," Josekanly said. "She needs to be reminded of who exactly it is who supports her. The common people. Those without magic."

"I have never thought of it that way," the king said, nodding.

A quiet knock on the door interrupted them.

The king's next appointment was here. Ozlandia, the head of the guards, probably with more bad news.

"I'm sorry, that's all the time I have for you today," the king said. He actually did regret having to send the troll on his own. "Could you come and talk with me again? In a few days' time?"

Josekanly's eyes grew large. "That would be such an incredible honor, sire. Thank you. Thank you."

He kept bowing, again and again, as he backed out of the room.

What a pleasant encounter! The king had felt much better in his study in the presence of the young troll. Truly remarkable.

He'd just have to think of a way to keep the youngster in court for a while.

CHAPTER FIFTEEN

"You're sure that the demons are going to attack the Risilodan?" Ozlandia asked Fleurdekan, the troll standing in front of her in her tiny office. "The world of the rowdy boys?"

He looked like a common farmer, with a roughly spun gray-wool shirt, brown pants with a ragged hem around the knees, and dirty straw sandals. He had jagged teeth and tusks, and kept his head shaved bald. Though he looked as strong as a common troll, he also had begun to develop something of a pot belly.

What worked against him were how wide-set and round his eyes were. They gave him the look of being perpetually surprised. He'd also developed a great goofy grin and a hearty laugh that disarmed most beings.

Fleurdekan wasn't a spy, nor a farmer, though he occasionally turned his hand to both. He primarily worked as a traveling merchant, selling jewelry and trinkets—that were probably stolen, though Ozlandia had never been able to prove it—to rich farmers who lived outside of the main city.

Ozlandia and others in the king's guard let him continue his operation as long as he never tried to make too large of a score. He also brought them useful information on a regular basis.

Fleurdekan had been expanding his operation with Ozlandia's blessing to include selling some items to *kith and kin* races outside of Trollville. He'd been a lot more useful in collecting information that way.

"Yes, ma'am, I'm certain," Fleurdekan said, nodding and scratching behind his ear with dirty claws. "The two…merchants…were talking about how they were not moving their business back to the Risilodan world. They had it on good authority that the demons were going to attack there—possibly in as little as a week's time. Now, these two would sell their own mother to make a profit." He gave her that disarming grin. "Greedy thieves. They know they'd make a killing if they moved into the market at this point. They're planning on waiting two weeks, possibly three, until the dust settles. Then they'll move in."

Ozlandia stood up from behind her desk. "Thank you," she said, handing Fleurdekan a small pouch with gold in it. "You did the right thing coming to see me right away."

"I know we're not always on the same side," Fleurdekan said, suddenly serious. "But I figured that any information about demons and where they might be attacking is worth telling you about, and quickly." He shook his head. "Demons are just bad for business."

Ozlandia thanked Fleurdekan again and sent him on his way. She had to find Kizalynn. Now.

It did, but didn't, surprise Ozlandia that the demons had decided to attack the world of the rowdy boys again, so soon after the demons had had their asses handed to them in the first battle there. No one would be expecting them to attack that world again, not so soon.

It was time to get a little more payback. Show those damned demons that they weren't guaranteed to win the Great War.

* * *

Ozlandia found Kizalynn in the palace, in the room where she normally met with her generals. A huge table took up the center of the room, covered with maps of the various *kith and kin* worlds. Too many of those maps showed countries with red boaders, places where the races had changed alliances and were now friendly to the demons.

Kizalynn stood alone in the room, supposedly studying the maps in front of her, but Ozlandia suspected she'd just been resting. Not sleeping on the floor, though she looked tired enough to do that. She wore her dress uniform, the one she'd never worn into battle, so the metal rings sewn into the blue vest still shone and the outfit didn't smell like gore.

"What is it?" Kizalynn asked, looking up. "You have news."

Her voice sounded almost dead. Was she that exhausted? Or was it something else?

"I just received credible word that the demons are planning on going back to the world of the rowdy boys," Ozlandia told her.

That news settled like a twenty-pound weight across Kizalynn's shoulders. "I was just looking at where I could draw troops from," she said, sliding one map on top of another.

Ozlandia realized that new markings had been added to the various maps, showing concentrations of troll troops.

"Have you heard the newest edict from the king?" Kizalynn said, shifting her gaze back to the maps in front of her.

Ozlandia swallowed against a suddenly dry throat. She'd forgotten after hearing the news from Fleurdekan. "I have." The king had ordered half the king's guard back to protect Trollville, instead of keeping them where they would be most useful, fighting the war.

Suddenly, some of the worry that had been weighing Kizalynn down transferred itself to Ozlandia.

"I have an idea," Kizalynn said. "You're not going to like it."

"Tell me," Ozlandia said, bracing herself.

Kizalynn looked up. "Give the troops the option. They can give up their commission, leave the king's guard, and stay and fight. Or they can stay in the guard and come back here, where there are no battles. I have enough gold, barely, to continue paying them myself privately."

Ozlandia opened and shut her mouth a few times, the words not coming. "You're right," she finally said. "I don't like it. It feels like a cheat. Like we're obeying exactly what the king has asked of us, instead of fulfilling his will."

She didn't add that it felt like a demon trick, though that was exactly what it reminded her of.

"I know," Kizalynn said. "I understand. Believe me, I don't want to do this. But it's the only way I can see through this mess. We need the troops where they are."

Ozlandia shook her head. "Don't make me do this," she said. "Don't make me choose between my loyalty to the king and my loyalty to you. Because I'll always choose the king. I'm the head of the king's guard."

"I know," Kizalynn said. "Thank you for being honest with me," she added. "However, if you won't give the troops this choice, I will. And I will make sure that they know what you prefer, that they stay in the guard."

"You can't do this," Ozlandia said. "It isn't right." How could she stop Kizalynn? Her thoughts raced, even as the conflict built about whether or not she should even try.

Kizalynn's fist slamming down onto the table made her start.

"I know it isn't right," Kizalynn growled. "But pulling the troops isn't right either. He's only doing it because he's been so influenced by demons. He's taking their gold."

Ozlandia kept herself very still. She'd heard the rumors about that, of course, that the gold being used to pay the troops still had a taint to it.

And there were all the weapons that the king supplied, the cursed blades and axes. The blacksmiths had been working around the clock to melt down all the old weapons, purify the metals, then recast them.

She couldn't admit that though. Not out loud. Not without being disloyal to the king.

Maybe if she had proof… And more than just the fact that some of the gifts in the hall of viewing bore demonic corruption crystals.

"I won't stop you," Ozlandia said slowly. "But you'll need to move quickly." Because eventually, Ozlandia would have to move.

Kizalynn stared at her intently for three heartbeats. Was she about to try something stupid like attack? Or even to see if her authority stretched far enough to remove Ozlandia from her position?

"I honor your allegiance to the king," Kizalynn said after a few long moments. "I can only hope that your sense of duty keeps you warm after the bodies have started piling up."

Kizalynn marched out of the room without another word, probably heading directly back to the portal room to go and speak with the first of the troops.

Ozlandia sighed deeply. She knew her duty. She'd sworn an oath to the king and had upheld it throughout her service.

She never wanted to have to choose between the king and Kizalynn. Though deep in her heart, she'd always suspected that this day would come.

CHAPTER SIXTEEN

Buddy couldn't believe the report his minion had prepared and read out loud to him. (What was the point of being a prince of hell if you couldn't make your minions distill down the massive tomes that Lars generated into mere bullet points that even someone in upper management could understand?)

It seemed as though Lars' plan was working. On many of the worlds, the troll troops were being removed. Then, like dominos, the *kith and kin* races who were defending planes that weren't their own left as soon as the trolls did.

Buddy dismissed the minion in front of him with a promise of less spicy tacos for dinner as a reward and settled further into the chair behind his cool marble desk. With a flick of his talons, he dimmed the lights in his study, the gray-and-black concrete tiles covering the walls taking on a somber hue.

It should have made Buddy chortle with glee that Lars was succeeding—that he was making such a comeback after the disastrous battle with that damned princess troll.

However, Buddy felt disquieted. It was an uncomfortable feeling. It was the sort of feeling that he should engender in other beings, not feel it himself.

Buddy had been a prince of hell long enough to take these sorts of urges seriously. He patted his potbelly stomach and swung his feet up onto his solid desk to see if he could think things through.

He snorted at himself. Really? A demon like him spending serious time contemplating consequences? A year ago, even six months previously, even a suggestion that Buddy might do that sort of thing would have ended up with whoever had said it being tortured by Buddy's prodigious farts.

Lars had infected him, though. Seeing plans that worked had made Buddy more open to planning himself. Hell, he even had some pretty effective plans in place if Lars did manage to win the Great War.

Or even if he didn't.

What exactly was disturbing Buddy about the troop movements? Was there a pattern in the worlds being attacked (or not) that was upsetting? Something that his subconscious was seeing?

It wasn't as if the worlds being abandoned by the trolls and the *kith and kin* had any special meaning. They weren't closer or further away from Hell, as Hell was always just around the corner. The demonic troops being sent in to clean things up weren't different or special either.

It hurt Buddy's head to try to think of all of these things, the actions and consequences. Maybe he was just unsettled because Lars was so much closer to winning the Great War again.

That wasn't it. No, it had something specifically to do with the trolls. How quickly Lars had managed to get them to turn against each other.

Of course, trolls were notoriously fickle and stupid. Never keeping their promises.

Except…

Except that it hadn't been quick. Not at all. Lars had been slowly but steadily influencing and corrupting the court of the trolls since day one. Even before that. He'd started while he'd been in prison. His minions had been hard at work, spreading his influence.

Why would Lars have only focused his energies on the troll court?

No, he must have been doing the same with the other princes of hell at the same time.

Buddy thought that he knew who his friends were among the other princes (few) as well as his enemies (many).

Could Buddy actually count on anyone other than himself in the coup that Lars was surely planning once he sensed victory?

It wasn't that Buddy actually trusted any of the other demons. They were demons. Still, he'd found himself lulled by the lack of infighting that had been going on recently, as everyone's aggression had been sopped up by fighting in the war itself.

Or had it been? Had Lars been able to get the princes to cooperate with each other for the time being? So that no one would expect the knives when they came out?

Buddy suddenly saw a pattern among the other princes of hell, the ones who'd stopped fighting each other and turned all their aggression toward the war. It was a group of minor princes, not the major ones like Buddy himself, who had grown the quietest.

They would form a powerful contingent if they managed to stay allied through the end of the war.

Buddy found himself on his feet, pacing the solid concrete floor of his study, growling. He'd grown in size as well, his pocked and blemished skin turning sleek and red, his wings taking form out of shadows, his great talons slashing out at the walls. Fire rumbled in his belly and smoke drifted up from his nostrils, filling the air with a sense of impending doom.

He would *not* be deposed by an upstart demon like Lars. Even if that youngster knew how to plan and organize. Buddy was a big enough demon to admit that the coalition Lars had formed was pretty formidable. That group could topple most of the rest of the princes, overthrow the entire chain of command.

Buddy wasn't one for taking such a challenge lying down, though. Particularly not when his own precious skin was involved.

No, it would take a bribe here, a sly word there, to turn the allegiance of the princes back to where it belonged, either to their own selfish black hearts and worst impulses, or to Buddy, which was almost the same thing.

Buddy found himself shrinking back down to his less formidable size. He gave a good belch as the fire in his belly dissipated, blowing the smoke back up toward the ceiling. The lamps hanging from the walls suddenly lit back up, brightening the entire room.

It was time to throw a party. No one could throw a party like a prince of hell.

He'd have to keep the date fluid, always changing it due to circumstances beyond his control. Hint at its importance for Lars. Get him focused on the damned event. Keep him off his guard.

Turn Lars' attention away from the other princes while Buddy planted his doubt and discord among them.

Humming, Buddy left his study, heading toward the kitchen. He knew he'd promised less spicy tacos for dinner, but what was his word if it wasn't made to be broken?

CHAPTER SEVENTEEN

Vern looked up when the words on the page he was trying to read suddenly became unclear.

Huh. What was that?

He glanced up. The lights in the shop had just dimmed. He was about to automatically adjust the brightness back up to something comfortable when he remembered why the lights had abruptly gone down.

It was time to go home for dinner. Before he'd rigged the lights to dim this way, he'd ignored any alarm that he set and had disappeared until Lizzie had to send Christine to come and fetch him.

Vern had been spending all his days in the shop, reading the books that Nik had left behind, learning the intricacies of running a magic shop. As well as doing research on the blue nodule, learning the pieces of the complicated spell that Nik had created to stop all external influences.

The magical council had been very interested at first—they'd never seen such an effective spell. However, it was hideously expensive in terms of ingredients and time. Plus, the effect was so small for such effort—a single individual. It simply wasn't cost effective for them to try to replicate it.

However, Vern had discovered it to be very handy, even though he hadn't opened the shop up yet. Their home was protected—Vern had strengthened those charms as soon as he'd learned how—as were their cars. Still, it was as if a huge spider sat just out of sight, casting stray trails of influence toward him like webbing on a regular basis.

As if the demons were angling for any hearts or souls they could catch in their great webs.

The political climate sometimes made Vern feel as though they'd already won. So much hate was being cast upon anyone who was different, people who had different loves or skin color or religion.

He had to remind himself that the demons had not won. The struggle went on.

He closed up his current book—really, so many spells to learn! And ingredients!

The shop was shaping up nicely. He'd already ordered some of the standards that Nik had always carried, like silk bags for holding magical sachets, crystals that would grow into protective wards, even the magical chalk used for demarking circles of power.

There were things, though, that Vern wouldn't handle. In particular, a lot of the ingredients that went into demonic magic, like the live creatures, as well as the guaranteed fresh, steaming entrails.

No. Vern didn't have to maintain the same neutrality

that Nik had. He could run a strictly human magic shop. He actually liked the idea of that, working with other human magicians.

But for now, it was time to close up and go back home.

Vern quickly opened a portal, then stepped out of the shop and onto a pier that was close to his home over on Lake Washington. He and Lizzie had bought a condo down in Madison Park—something they never could have afforded on their own, if not for the inheritance that Lizzie had received just after they'd been married. It hadn't been that big when there were four of them, but now, with just two of them, it felt perfectly cozy.

Smiling, Vern stepped off the wooden pier onto solid land. Rain pattered down softly, more like mist than drops. The air felt soft and warm, and smelled of wet grass. Vern was looking forward to the rains really starting, but he was happy with the fall so far, the bright days and amazing colors.

There were still a few supplies he had to get in before he'd open the shop. He'd agreed with Dennis to start with a "soft" opening, with unreliable hours for two weeks before the official grand opening. That way he could get his feet wet, see what supplies he ran out of right away, and so on.

Should he order more of the generic healing potions? Nik had gone through whatever he stocked quickly enough, in part, because of the war. Should he bring in some bandages and more mundane stock for healing? He just wasn't sure.

Vern was so involved with thinking about supplies that

he almost missed the first call. It felt far away, as if someone back on the pier had called out to him.

He stopped and concentrated.

There it was again. A word, off in the distance.

"Shopkeeper."

With it came a foul stench, as though something had rolled in dog shit then let it bake into their filthy fur.

Without hesitation, Vern pulled out his wand and set up a shield spell around him.

Sure enough, a group of half a dozen demons came strolling up the sidewalk toward him. They had a curious gait, as if they were more used to walking on four legs rather than two. Pointed snouts with sharp teeth grinned at him. They had human-like bodies, though their hands were long and thin, the backs covered in spotted fur, their fingers tipped in dirty claws.

Vern would guess they were some strain of hyena. They chittered amongst themselves as they approached him, and a couple had pointed ears standing up on the top of matted, greasy hair.

"What do you want?" Vern asked. He figured he should at least start out friendly.

They'd learn quickly enough what would happen if they decided to push.

A brief wave of cold washed over him, as if he'd been standing in the sunlight and had just passed through a shadow.

Once again, Vern thanked Nik for the anti-influence spell.

"So. We hears youse gonna open up the shop again. Nik's place," said what appeared to be the leader. He wore a stained army jacket that bulged over his belly, though the rest of him appeared thin and lean.

Vern would guess that had to do with the conservation of mass—that the beings in front of him were actually much larger in their demon form.

"That's correct," Vern said. "Eventually."

Again that wave of shadow passing over him.

"Youse wouldn't wanna give us a quick look, first like?" the leader said, leaning forward slightly.

Vern drew himself up. "You can come by when the shop is officially open. Not before," he said.

The leader looked puzzled. "You sure 'bout that? Human?"

A much stronger shadow pulsed over Vern this time, as if he'd just walked through a cloud filled with snow.

Vern gave them his best smile. "Absolutely. Dudes."

The demons glanced at each other, obviously not understanding why Vern wasn't just folding under their combined pressure.

"Oh, and by the way, you'll find that I'm as immune to influence as Nik was," Vern added. "You might want to spread the word."

"How's that possible?" the lead demon asked.

"Nik crafted the spell for me," Vern said. He figured that was the right thing to tell them, as every being knew that Nik had been above all influence.

"Ah," the leader said, nodding. "But what if we mix it up some?"

Without warning, the leader slashed out with one of his claws.

Vern felt the slash of the thing's claws against the

shield spell he'd already formed. Without hesitation, he called up an electrical attack, zinging first one creature, then the next, and so on, stringing the group together with a single sizzling bolt. He added a holding element to it, so that all the creatures were now standing frozen, though they shook with the current pouring through them.

"You can also let the others know that I'm not that vulnerable to that sort of thing either," Vern said sternly. "Anyone who tries a physical attack will fail, as you did. And be unwelcome to ever set foot in the store again."

Instead of just releasing them, Vern flung them to the side, sending them far out into the middle of the lake.

He didn't know if they could swim or not. He didn't care.

Vern hurried up to the door of his building. His hands were shaking so badly it took him three tries just to get his key into the lock of the door.

Once inside, he took a deep breath before walking to the staircase, then going up three flights to his home.

He knew he wasn't safe here, even though he'd reached the sanctity of his home. He'd never be safe, regardless of whether he went ahead and opened up the shop or not. He and the rest of the family were targets because of Christine.

He wasn't about to stop fighting the good fight though. At least both Christine and Ty had warned him that the demons would come sniffing around, looking for vulnerabilities.

Vern wasn't a fighter. He'd learned that first at the big battle with the obelisk of truth, then at the second skirmish that Christine had brought him into. He really was more suited to be a shopkeeper.

However, he wasn't a coward, even though he felt that way sometimes. He would always defend himself and his family.

Even if he would have to go and throw up afterward.

CHAPTER EIGHTEEN

DENNIS DIDN'T ALLOW HIMSELF TO EITHER CROW with delight, or even to do a fist pump, though he really wanted to.

Instead, he merely nodded, saying, "That's awesome!" He didn't care how goofy his smile was. He was overjoyed that Du Ko, the Longian sculptor, had managed to convince a second group of his people to join Christine's war effort.

Christine had let Dennis know that the Longians were amazing fighters after the first battle they'd been in, and that anything he could do to help bring more of them over would be a great service.

Dennis considered each and every *kith and kin* race who he managed to bring to the war effort to be a victory against the demons. That he'd convinced more Longians was just icing on the cake.

Du Ko and Dennis met at a coffee shop on the human plane. (Dennis has counted bringing Du Ko here to be his first major victory.)

Du Ko appeared as a very tall, lanky human male, with long black hair that fell over East Asian-looking eyes, a soft smile, and incredibly long hands. His skin was a light brown color, darker than most of the Asians Dennis knew, with pale tan palms. He tended to wear plain T-shirts—today's being a muted green color—with jeans and sandals.

He was very laid back as a human—literally that morning, with his legs stretched out under the table and leaning far back in his chair.

While Du Ko had used Dennis for his muse for a second piece, Dennis had always thought the Longian, himself, would make a great model. He had that artsy look to his face, and eyes that always appeared to be half-asleep, dreaming the really good dreams.

"I'll let Christine know," Dennis said.

"I assume that she'll want me to send them to the Risilodan world," Du Ko said.

"The Risilodan…You mean the rowdy boys?" Dennis asked, confused. The huge battle with the demons two weeks ago had happened there, and Christine had handed them their *asses*, thank you very much. "Why would the demons attack there?"

Du Ko shrugged. "I assume they always meant to go back, and couldn't get their act together to go sooner than this."

"I see," Dennis said, nodding. Did Christine know? Of course she did. She was always well informed about this sort of thing. "Yeah, if you think that's where they should go. I'll let you know if I hear otherwise."

"Good," Du Ko said. He pulled himself up to

standing. Dennis stood as well, always feeling as though he needed to grow some, or wear boots with a heel, whenever he met with the Longian.

Then again, the other being never made him uncomfortable. It was just his own head, and his old reactions to things.

They shook hands formally, then Du Ko turned and walked out of the shop.

Dennis sat back down, toying with his coffee cup. He composed a crowing letter in his head to Christine, talking about how awesome he was, how right she was for hiring him, how much the Longians would help.

He'd never send it, though. He knew that. She didn't need his selfish accolades. He was surprised at how well she did keep track of every being and race he recruited. Then again, she'd trained as a librarian. She probably had a system set up for these things.

Dennis had to laugh at himself. He remembered scoffing at the old adage that a job well done was reward enough. No, you needed to make sure that your bosses knew, and your boss's boss, as well as your co-workers and everyone on your team. You had to crow about your wins because sure as hell no one else would.

Technically, Dennis worked for Christine; however, as she was so hands-off, he felt as though he just worked for himself. And he'd turned out to be a much harder taskmaster than any of his former bosses.

He knew he'd done a good job, was doing the right thing. And honestly, that was enough, now.

Dennis picked up his phone and looked at the meetings he'd set up for the rest of the day.

Ugh. The next one was with the Poper Lei. They had a hive mind, and Dennis was never certain who would be representing their race that day. Sometimes it was Su No, a kindly old lady figure who rambled and called him dear. It was always difficult to get to the point with her. But other times it was Harvey, who looked, dressed, and smelled like a biker, of leather, cigarette smoke, and cheap cannabis. He was just as bad in terms of telling stories.

As Dennis had recruited more of the Longians, maybe he could postpone the meeting with the Poper Lei? Take the afternoon off?

That may have been what he would have done at his old day job. But it wasn't more than a passing thought now.

Instead, he decided to take himself to a really good steak dinner that night, to celebrate. Maybe he should invite the Peter, the Thothian, as part of his reward for doing all the cleansing work at the palace in Trollville?

Dennis sent him a text, knowing he wouldn't get it until he set foot on the human plane. After drinking the rest of his coffee, Dennis stood up again. He was debating going to his car and switching jackets—instead of the heavy raincoat, maybe he should pick up his leather coat —when a couple walked into the shop.

It took Dennis a moment to place the woman. She wore her blonde-brown hair back in a ponytail. Her skin almost looked golden in this light. She wore the brightest turquoise rain jacket that he'd ever seen. Her smile was radiant, momentarily blinding him.

That was Laurie. He remembered her now, from when he'd gone to see the oracles with Christine.

The man beside her also looked vaguely familiar, though Dennis couldn't remember his name. He wore a black leather biker vest over a short-sleeved T-shirt, showing full sleeves of tattoos. He had brown hair that fell into his eyes, much more pale skin than Laurie's, though they shared the same smile.

Laurie glanced over at Dennis, who gave her a big grin and nodded at her.

Her eyes grew large, as did her smile.

Was that her husband? Her boyfriend?

He'd never know unless he went over to ask.

"Hi. Laurie, right?" Dennis said as he walked up to her. His heart pounded surprisingly hard and his palms had started sweating.

God, her skin was *perfect*. He bet that it was that soft all over, too.

"That's right," she said softly. "You remember."

"I do," Dennis said. He'd forgotten about her after he'd visited the oracle. "I don't know how I could have forgotten someone as perfect as you."

Then he realized what he'd just said. He didn't blush—that wasn't his style. Still, he could recover from this. "I hope I didn't just embarrass you in front of your boyfriend."

"No, this is my cousin, Toby," Laurie said.

The young man turned toward Dennis. He had amazingly bright blue eyes.

"I'm Toby," the man said, holding out his hand for a remarkably firm handshake.

"Have we met?" Dennis said, still curious.

"Nope," Toby told him.

"I'm on my way to another meeting," Dennis told Laurie. "If you're not seeing anyone, I'd love to take you out for coffee tomorrow." His heart still felt as though it he'd run around the block to meet her, instead of just standing there. He normally wasn't this nervous. What the hell?

"I'm still single, yes," Laurie said, shooting a hard glare at Toby for a moment. "And I'd love to have coffee with you."

They set a time and place, Dennis quickly making the appointment in his calendar, as well as handing her a business card with his contact information on it. It listed his name, phone number, as well as two email addresses: one that was more "public" facing, that just anyone could find and use, a gmail account. The other was the one that the *kith and kin* favored, as if the private network made it easier.

"See you then," Dennis said. He turned away reluctantly. For some reason, he really didn't want to leave her presence.

He remembered Christine's reaction to Laurie. Hadn't Christine told him that Laurie was somehow related to the Host? To angels?

That would make perfect sense to Dennis, as Laurie seemed pretty perfect to him.

He left the coffeeshop with a tremendous grin on his face. Not only had he recruited more of the Longians, now he had a date with the most beautiful women he'd ever met.

Even the Poper Lei wouldn't be able to ruin this day.

CHAPTER NINETEEN

Christine was standing on one of the great plains of the rowdy boys' world when she felt the ground rumble. She didn't have to stretch her senses far to find a great hole opening up in the earth, about to belch out smoke and demons.

She'd been told that the world of the rowdy boys was always cool, the temperature never getting above seventy Fahrenheit, and only for a short time in the summer. When it wasn't winter and snowing, the air always held a crispness to it that reminded her of the best parts of fall.

Gray clouds covered the sky, hiding whatever sun and warmth that might have been. The rowdy boys were mostly farmers, so huge grassy plains covered most of their world, with a few forests thrown in for good measure. Well-built roads connected the farmsteads with the markets, but more importantly, with the arenas where their annual games took place.

The foul wind carrying the stench of the demons just

made her angry, reminding her of how they polluted everything they touched.

She looked to her left and right, at the small group of trolls who she fought with, maybe two dozen in all. That also left a bitter taste in her mouth.

When she'd told the guard about the edict from the king, as well as her solution, she'd assumed that half would stay.

Less than a quarter had, though. The majority of the trolls also chose to return to Trollville immediately, not even waiting a day.

Other *kith and kin* races followed suit, leaving entire worlds now vulnerable to demon attacks.

With a final nod, Christine raced forward with her laughably small troop. The rowdy boys would also fight—they'd been cornered, and would come out fiercely. Constenllo, their leader, had at one point hinted that they might have to change alliances and become allies with the demons.

That had been before the great clash on their world, between the huge demon armies and everyone who Christine could muster. There was no talk of switching loyalties now. The rowdy boys were pissed off that their world had become such a large battleground. They were still recovering from the event, as well as mourning the destruction of their largest playing field.

Which was why the demons chose to press their advantage, to try to take over the world again, to commit xenocide and kill all the remaining rowdy boys.

Fortunately, the rowdy boys wouldn't go down without a tremendous fight.

Christine gulped when her boots shook again and again. She could sense additional holes opening up in the good earth. The demons were pouring into the world.

No matter how fiercely her remaining fighters may battle, eventually they'd be overwhelmed by the sheer number of demons.

It didn't matter. She couldn't give up on the rowdy boys. Not yet.

Instead, she raced ahead, her great ax raised, ready to war.

CHRISTINE BOWLED OVER MORE DEMONS WITH HER wind power, sending them rolling back to the great hole that they came out of. She couldn't set them on fire, as the particular group of demons she fought seemed to have some sort of fire immunity, and it also bothered the rowdy boys.

She'd tried using her earth element to close the holes before the demons had started pouring out, to choke off their route, but the portal they traveled through was too powerful for her to close. She disrupted the demons, causing fissures to open up in the ground and swallow as many of them as she could manage.

Mainly though, she fought. At least the damned demons were no longer carrying the corruption crystals, so not only did her magical attacks work, she wasn't instantly struck with despair at the beginning of the battle.

No, the despair had crept up slowly as she lost good trolls and laughing rowdy boys to the filthy demons.

Christine slashed out with her ax, swinging it from side to side, slicing heads, arms, bodies. She was covered in grime and gore, the scent of battle sickeningly familiar. At least these demons seemed to be minor, minions thrown at them like a stream of rats into a fight.

More teeth flew as Christine knocked the nearest demon away. Two trolls fought at her side, good, well-trained guards who deserved a better fate than to be brought down by demons. They plowed through the stream of creatures coming at them. Only once in a while did one of the creatures bear a sword or shield. Mostly, they fought with wicked claws and snake-fast bites.

Christine felt herself tiring. And maybe that was the point. To exhaust her troops before the demons brought out the big guns.

Would she have to retreat? She was much stronger than she used to be, and the earth itself would give her strength.

Would dying on this plane help the war effort? No. She had to continue. She couldn't choose a place for her death. It would have to capture her unaware.

Christine fought on, desperate now. Her arms strained with the effort. Boots covered in blood and muck stomped down on the next body. She pivoted and slashed again, directing her mighty ax to the side.

At least her small group wasn't surrounded. Not yet. But the stream of filth pouring from the portal seemed unending.

Christine stepped back and let her two guards continue fighting while she directed more large rocks at the portal itself, dumping them into the opening, trying to at least stem the tide.

It seemed to work this time. Demons started trickling out, instead of a huge stream racing toward them.

A horn sounded in the distance, one of those obnoxious bellowing things that the demons used to rally their troops.

Damn it! That meant more demons. More fighting. More good trolls dying.

Christine turned back to the fight in front of her, determined not to die at this point, to call the retreat before it was too late.

The earth rumbled again.

Christine fought on despite her despair.

CHAPTER TWENTY

Ty had been surprised when Malcom, the human magician, had contacted him. They didn't operate in the same circles. Malcom was on the magical council and trained young magicians. While Ty had magic, his wasn't human based.

He'd met Malcom at one of the parties Christine had thrown, or her parents, rather. Of course, they'd been the only two African-Americans at the party, though not the only people of color. And Ty hadn't been the only being who wasn't fully human.

But Malcom had heard about Ty's training, and had a young magician who was struggling with their own inner demons. Ty had never talked much about it before telling the council. It wasn't anyone's damned business but his own. However, for the war effort, Ty was willing to forgo his usual reticence and tell his story in the hopes that it might help someone else.

They met at a trendy wine bar down in Georgetown, south of downtown. Ty figured Malcom had chosen that place because it was close to where the struggling magician lived.

The bar itself was divided into two parts. The front half was a huge room filled with dozens of pinball machines. A solid wall of sound struck Ty when he walked in the door: electronic pings, whizzing ball noises, theme music, and laughter. The blinking lights of the machines brightly colored the room, highlighting the young people standing there in garish colors. Though the night air outside was delightfully cool, the front room was humid and stank of sweat and cheap alcohol.

Ty quickly wove around the machines, feeling as though all his senses were being bludgeoned, making his way to the bar in the back.

Fortunately, a solid wall separated the two rooms, holding most of the noise at bay. The back was tiny, with low lights and a bar that ran all the way along the left. A dozen small tables surrounded by chairs filled the rest of the space. While the front room was full, with groups playing almost every machine, the back only had three tables with people at them.

Ty spotted Malcom sitting in the far corner with… Tina? Christine's human doppelganger?

He waved at them, then went to order a porter that they had on tap, figuring this counted as dessert. It also gave him time to think.

Why was Tina there?

Ty had met Tina at more than one of the Sunday dinners that the Tuckermans had thrown over the years, since they considered him part of the family. Ty had never had much use for Tina. She always struck him as a princess who'd never had to grow up. Everything had always been handed to her.

Plus, Tina had turned on Christine on more than one occasion. Ty didn't trust her.

Still, Ty put on a smile as he walked with his full pint over to the table. He took a seat and nodded to both of them, letting them talk first.

"I'm assuming you know each other," Malcom said after they'd all said hi. "So no introductions need be made."

"Yes," Tina said cautiously. "Is this the being you were telling me about?"

"It is," Malcom said proudly. "Do you know Ty's background?"

Tina shrugged. "I'd always assumed that you were *kith and kin*. Malcom says you're not."

"I'm part lycanthrope," Ty admitted. He realized he'd never told her or any of the Tuckermans, not even Christine.

"Really?" Tina asked.

Ty had to admit she seemed adequately surprised.

"But you don't—I mean, you're not cursed, are you? I've seen you on the full moon," she said. Even in the dim light Ty could see her confusion.

Ty explained about his heritage, as well as how he'd trained to keep that part of him in check.

"Wow," Tina said, her eyes huge. "Would this work for a full-blood lycanthrope?"

"It would," Ty said. "I've actually met a few. They stay hidden, though. The one who you might call out and proud is shunned by the community." He shrugged. "It's more difficult for them than it is for me. Then again, they also started training older than I did."

"Huh," Tina said. She appeared lost in thought for a few moments, sipping her glass of what appeared to be an overly sweet wine spritzer. She glanced up, caught Malcom's eye, and nodded.

"I've been corrupted by demons," she said, her voice sounding surprisingly matter-of-fact about it. "More than once. They've tainted my soul. This last time, I tapped into that demonic power." She stared at him. "Dark magic. Powerful. Black."

Ty blinked, surprised. While he wasn't familiar with the inner workings of human magicians, he was aware that human magic was mostly powered by the Host, which tended to make it clean and light.

He couldn't actually think of any humans whose magic was demonic in nature, or who dabbled in what the myths called black magic.

"My adoptive parents think it's a phase, that I'll get over it if they just send me to enough shrinks," Tina continued.

Ty shared an eyeroll with her. Good luck with that.

"I need to learn how to balance my magic, so that the demonic-fueled power doesn't take over the other parts," she said. "Just ignoring it is the surest way for it to drown me."

"Interesting," Ty said, intrigued despite his reservations. "So what are you looking for?" He wanted to make sure that whatever agreement they reached was all spelled out.

"I want help learning how to balance," she said. "To

only allow the demon power out when I need it, to be in control of it, and not let it take over."

Ty pressed his lips together while he thought. He'd never taken on a student. Wasn't even sure he knew how to teach what he already knew.

"When I went and talked to the council, I'd assumed that they'd contact *my* masters, the beings I learned from. Not me, directly," he said.

"Yeah, but I know you," Tina said. "And Christine trusts you."

Ty nodded at her, hearing the unspoken truth: Tina didn't necessarily trust Ty any more than he trusted her.

"And I know you both," Malcom said quietly. "I think you'd work well together."

Ty raised an eyebrow at that, but didn't say anything. He and Malcom didn't know each other that well.

Then again, Malcom was a lot more than he appeared. It wouldn't surprise Ty to learn that Malcom had a touch of the Host in him.

Ty finally spoke up. "You know that when Christine brought me to you to be healed, you actually messed me up much more."

Tina grew stiff, but eventually she nodded. "I didn't. Or I did, but I hadn't thought about it. I'm sorry. I shouldn't have tried, but sent Christine on to the healer right away."

Ty was impressed that she didn't make any excuses to him, though he could tell that she wanted to.

"All right," Ty said eventually. "We don't necessarily trust each other, but that's okay. Trust can be earned. Particularly since we can be honest with each other. As long as we keep that up, I think we might have a chance."

"I can be as brutally honest as you need me to be," Tina said with a wry grin. "That has been something the shrinks have been helping me with."

Interesting. Possibly Tina was turning into someone who Ty wanted to get to know. They set a schedule for meeting before Ty finished his porter and went on his way.

Maybe something good would come out of the war.

If they survived.

CHAPTER TWENTY-ONE

WHAT THE HELL?

Christine stared in amazement as trolls came streaming up out of the earth and onto the open plane of the world of the rowdy boys.

The trolls weren't armed with the good axes of the king's guard. Nor did they wear uniforms.

Instead, they carried wooden pikes, ancient swords, and even scythes used to harvest grain. They wore the common clothes of farmers, roughly spun shirts, vests, and pants.

The roar they gave as they streamed toward the field of battle was greater than she'd ever heard before. It resonated deeply in her chest, making her heart beat faster.

She knew that the humans had been experimenting with portals, seeing if they could replicate the work of the demons. They couldn't corrupt an eruption spell—corruption was a demon trick. It seemed as though they'd managed something similar, as the air smelled of good dirt and not waste and filth.

As the first wave of trolls engaged with the endless streams of demons, she realized that despite how they looked, these weren't common trolls, no, they were trained to fight.

It took her a moment to put it all together.

These were the king's guard. They hadn't abandoned her. They'd gone back to Trollville to officially resign their commissions, turn in their weapons and their uniforms, before they came back to fight.

They'd brought their brothers and sisters as well, trolls who weren't as well trained but who were just as tough.

And just as angry.

Ozlandia had told Christine more than once that she'd take a small group of untrained trolls over a legion of the *kith and kin* any day.

Seemed she was right.

Christine helped the trolls in their slaughter with her magic, battering away enemies with her winds, dropping stones on some, freezing others.

For the first time since the start of the war, Christine saw the tide turn. The demons around her didn't realize what was happening, and so didn't call a retreat. Maybe they'd been fooled by the rumbling ground and had thought more demons were coming.

The trolls took the field, the entire battleground. None of the demons near Christine made it back through the massive portal.

Additional skirmishes raged to Christine's left and right. Her "troops" professionally divided themselves and engaged with the enemy without her direction. They'd fought long enough under the king's colors to know what to do.

Only now did she hear the call for retreat from the demons, finally pulling back from the field.

She knew she hadn't won the war. Not yet. Lars was still out there with his plans and his tricks. It still surprised her that he'd never shown up that day. He would have some trick planned for her, for when they did meet.

No matter.

She'd deal with him later.

For now, she had cause to celebrate.

CHAPTER TWENTY-TWO

L ARS FUMED AS HE WAITED OUTSIDE B UDDY'S STUDY. He had a *war* to run, thank you very much. This morning's battle was when Lars would finally wipe out the rowdy boys, sweep them from the field, then go and hunt them down on every plane where they tried to hide.

Make an example of them, show all the races of the *kith and kin* that no matter how big or how small, the demons would get you, and you would lose in the end.

But Buddy had assured Lars that this would be a short meeting, as most of them were. Lars could still make an appearance on the field of battle after his troops had softened up the resistance.

Lars blinked, confused when Buddy himself opened the door to his study at the appointed time, instead of making Lars wait as he usually did.

"Won't you come in?" Buddy said, sounding pleased instead of completely pissed off.

Lars stayed where he was for a moment, struck dumb by the implications.

Not only was Buddy on time, he hadn't sent a minion to fetch Lars, but had opened the door himself.

Though those might seem like insignificant acts, Lars knew they were hugely important.

Finally! It was about time that Buddy woke up and smelled the brimstone. Lars was *winning* the Great War. He wasn't about to fail. It was only his due that the princes of hell fete him properly.

He swelled up with pride, nodded his head graciously, then walked across the threshold.

Into a version of hell that he'd never imagined before.

The room was still the same, with plain gray concrete tiles covering the walls and floor, stalagmites that dripped cold, slimy water at the least convenient of times, as well as Buddy's magnificent marble desk at the far end of the space.

However, stations had been set up all around the room, each with a different festive display, going from ridiculous white snowflakes and pink bubbles to full-on lava and brimstone. Hell, there was even one that had both snowflakes and lava.

"These are all the various party themes my minions came up with," Buddy explained excitedly. "I had so many ideas! I couldn't choose between them. Since this is *your* victory party, I figured you'd want a say in the final decorations."

The balloons, glitter, bubbling vats of mud, and scent of raw entrails all caused Lars' head to swim.

Shouldn't his minions be making these choices? Just bring three of the top designs for Lars to choose? Was this actually how the princes of hell spent their time? Arranging flowers?

"I see," Lars said. He looked around the room, then back at Buddy, who gave him a wide, disarming grin.

"I know that you have a war to run, but this won't take much time at all. It's too important a task to delegate," Buddy assured him. "It's your party, after all."

"All right," Lars said, mollified. He could do this. Then get back to the world of the rowdy boys, and slay that damned princess troll once and for all.

LARS MARCHED ANGRILY DOWN ONE OF THE ENDLESS corridors of hell. He cursed Buddy silently, not out loud—curses had strength, particularly when spoken by a strong demon while he was actually in hell. And Lars wasn't ready to curse a prince of hell.

Yet.

One of the funny things about hell was that Lars could never really tell how long he was down there. His own internal clock never worked right and he couldn't rely on anything manufactured.

Plus, Buddy had made sure that the time had stretched on and on. Lars wasn't sure how Buddy had managed to sound both interesting as well as nail-bitingly boring at the exact same time. It was a skill that Lars had yet to acquire.

It was obvious though, in hindsight, that Buddy had intended to torture Lars all morning long, to keep his attention focused on the damned party that was being given in his honor.

Was it just Buddy's nature? That he kept tweaking Lars' nose, as it were? That had to be part of it. Buddy couldn't help but torture those who were around him. It was the nature of his being.

Possibly Buddy had some ulterior motive for keeping Lars in hell for that long. However, as Buddy hadn't left the room once, Lars couldn't figure out what it was. He'd been stuck in there with Lars the entire time, filling the room with his noxious farts and vile jokes.

Lars had discovered that even he had a limit when it came to crude puns and limericks.

And now, Lars had even worse news. His demons had suffered a humiliating defeat at the hands of the damned trolls on the world of the rowdy boys. He wasn't exactly sure what had happened. Some troll regiment or another had returned. It was impossible to get an accurate count of the force the demons had faced, as all of his generals tended to exaggerate.

If only Lars had been there!

Now, instead of the demons winning and hunting the few remaining rowdy boys down, that damned princess troll had gone on the offense, following the demons back to their staging world. A bloody battle still raged, with the demons losing.

It just would not do.

However, Lars wasn't about to go set foot there himself. Why take a chance on being injured? Sure, his troops would rally when he did make an appearance. But the odds were against him, and Lars wasn't about to go into a fight only to have to call a retreat.

He'd just lose this batch of demons. They weren't his

weakest fighters, but were close to it. He shouldn't have been trying to overwhelm the rowdy boys with sheer numbers. Next time, he'd choose a heartier contingent to attack them with.

In the meanwhile, he needed to get back to his official headquarters on earth, pick up the pieces, and put his next plans into place.

CHAPTER TWENTY-THREE

The king nodded sorrowfully at Josekanly as he took another sip of the excellent dark beer that they served at Tanner's Way, the small commoner's pub that he'd first gone to when meeting with Manny.

Garethen wore his typical disguise, tinting his skin darker, less green, than normal, white hair that was trimmed around his neck instead of long and flowing, and gold caps on the ends of his two lower tusks. He kept his clothing simple as well, with a common long-sleeved white shirt—the kind that merchants wore—as well as plain gray wool trousers and comfortable straw sandals.

Josekanly had met him at the tavern that night, also praising their excellent beer. He, too, wore common clothing instead of his fine court wear, along with a cap to hide his short hair.

"I hadn't expected such disloyalty," the king muttered as he took another sip. He'd ordered the king's guard back. That they'd come in such numbers had heartened him.

He'd thought that meant that they were loyal to him.

Then they'd started resigning, one after another. He'd heard reports of a huge line forming out the door of Ozlandia's office and down three hallways. They'd all left the guard, even veterans with decades of experience. At least he hadn't had to pay out full pension to them, or he really would have gone broke. They'd been willing to take an annual remittance instead of a large lump sum.

Maybe he'd be able to tax that later, so he wouldn't have to pay it all out.

That afternoon, he'd learned that instead of going back to their families and their farms, the troops had gathered together for a short while on the human world, posing as large tour groups, only to be transported back into battle.

He couldn't order the trolls away. They were no longer part of the king's guard. And he couldn't order Kizalynn not to use them. She had the right to staff her army with any and all available trolls.

Still, it irritated him, how they'd disobeyed him and proven to be so disloyal.

"It's shocking, that they all went back to fight for *her*," Josekanly muttered. He generally referred to Kizalynn just as *her* anymore. "Don't they have any self-respect?"

"Aye," the king said, agreeing after another sip of beer. "She must have bribed them," he added in a low voice.

Josekanly's eyes grew wide. "She has her own fortune, doesn't she?"

The king nodded. "Family money. Not from me. She hasn't gotten a single copper penny from me. Though she's taken plenty from me already."

He still mourned every time he passed by the almost empty hall of viewing. He had to admit that the number of corrupted items had surprised him. He'd demanded a presentation from that ugly Thothian, proving that the gifts had been corrupted.

It hadn't taken long to arrange. The greasy smoke that rose up from each one that was touched with a holy item from the human Host had turned Garethen's stomach.

In a moment of weakness, he'd granted Kizalynn the right to contact the merchants who'd provided the goods, to make sure that they'd been innocent in the affair and hadn't knowingly been supplying the king and the court with tainted goods.

It had made the mood in the city ugly. Not only were their young men being sent off to battle and being killed by demons, now the damned demons had infected the merchants as well. The king had been grateful for the few guards who had remained in the service after returning from the battlefields, just so they could protect him.

Not that the common troll would ever think of storming the palace. The king was safe there.

But the trolls were angry. Even here, in Tanner's Way, there was a dark undercurrent to the room. The usual quartet wasn't in the corner, singing, and no one was playing drunken darts. Instead, groups of trolls clustered tightly together, drinking and muttering.

"And now she's wasting more good trolls' lives," Josekanly said, shaking his head in disgust. "Can't you order her back to the palace?"

The younger troll had asked that before. Each time, Garethen had come up with a different reason why he couldn't.

Tonight, it was finally time for the truth.

"I could order her home," the king said quietly. "Threaten her inheritance if she doesn't obey. That sort of thing."

"Really?" Josekanly said, his dark eyes wide. "Then why don't you?"

King Garethen sighed and took another sip of his beer. "Because she wouldn't obey me. She'd leave me, and I'd be all alone, as I was for all those years before she returned. Because I don't have another heir who's worthy."

"Is such a disloyal heir truly worthy?" Josekanly asked quietly.

"That's the question, eh?" Garethen acknowledged. "She has been the right choice before now." He threw an appraising glance at the young troll beside him.

Even in a commoner disguise, it was apparent that Josekanly was anything but common. He had a presence to him that the king couldn't help but recognize, a quality that made him stand out. In addition to a fine physique, he looked distinguished in a way that the king understood was the royal blood that Josekanly carried.

And though the young man certainly had a way about him, an undeniable charm, Garethen could never overlook the troll's completely mundane nature.

Royalty needed magic. An unmagical king or queen wouldn't be able to properly run the palace. That was all there was to it. As much as the king like Josekanly, he couldn't bring himself to promote the young troll to the level of an heir.

As a potential bridegroom, however…

Josekanly stood up straighter at Garethen's look. "It

would be my honor to fulfill any position you may bestow upon me."

Garethen merely nodded and sipped his beer. He wasn't convinced. Not yet. "Let's go play some darts," he proposed instead.

Such weighty conversations could take place later.

GARETHEN WAS SURPRISED NOT ONLY AT HOW WELL he was throwing darts, but at how much fun he was having.

He hadn't remembered having this much fun in an age or more.

"More beer!" he roared, handing Josekanly his mug while he lined up his next shot. They had quite a crowd gathered around them, placing casual bets both for and against Garethen.

He'd show them.

He wore a blindfold, as a troll could generally always hit whatever he or she aimed at. One of the other fellows, Andreseki, turned Garethen around quickly, trying to confuse him, make him lose his target.

Garethen wasn't cheating. Not exactly. But he did have magic, while the rest of these poor bastards didn't have a clue.

Without a care, Garethen turned his head toward the target and tossed his dart that way.

It didn't have to hit the bullseye. Just somewhere near the target.

The way the crowd grew quiet around him surprised

him.

Garethen lifted the blindfold off one eyes and glanced around him. The dart had sunk deep into the target, just one ring out from the bullseye.

"How did you do that?" Andreseki asked, looking confused. "You threw it in the wrong direction. Then the dart just kind of circled around and found the target."

"He's got magic," one of the female trolls proclaimed. "I bet he's a royal."

The hush that had just been immediately around Garethen extended throughout the room, now.

He didn't see how he could deny it. Or even if he should. These were good trolls here. Surely they deserved to know the truth?

"You are correct," Garethen said, straightening up. "I am, as you said, one of the royals."

He let his disguise melt away, revealing that their king stood among them.

The crowd whispered his name as he stood proudly, reveling in their awe.

Unfortunately, it didn't last long.

"Why'd you order the guards back?" Andreseki said. "My son was happy in the king's guard. Happy to be fighting. You made him come back here."

"You're denying our children their chance at battle scars," another troll said. "They need their own stories to tell their children."

King Garethen blinked, surprised. He'd thought his subjects would approve of him bringing the troops back home. "They were dying needlessly," he said scornfully. "We need them here to protect us."

"What, ye think we can't fight?" a woman asked. She looked as though she'd been in more than one battle herself, with one of her tusks broken and a scar running from her left ear down along the side of her face. "Whoever thinks they can take a country of trolls is sadly mistaken."

That brought a hearty cheer.

King Garethen shook his head, sorry that he'd allowed himself the indulgence of taking off his disguise. Then again, what did these trolls know of war? Most of their scars probably came from tavern brawls.

"Thank you for your hospitality," the king said, nodding his head regally at them. "And thank you for the beer," he added, with an additional nod at the barkeep.

The dark beer here really had been excellent. Shame he wouldn't be able to come back.

Josekanly also dropped his disguise and came to stand beside the king, tall and proud. Garethen knew they struck quite a picture, and that their appearance would be talked about for a long time.

Maybe it was time to legitimize his relationship with Josekanly. Propose an agreement for the merger of their houses. Kizalynn wouldn't like it, but she didn't appear to like anything the king suggested these days.

He couldn't order her to marry Josekanly. However, perhaps he could talk her into it, particularly if he gave her more troops.

Arm in arm, Garethen and Josekanly walked out into the soft night, making their slow way back to the palace, both silent with their own plans and schemes.

CHAPTER TWENTY-FOUR

"That's the last one," Ozlandia's assistant, Cactimakus, said, sticking his head in the door of Ozlandia's tiny office.

"Thank you," Ozlandia said as she closed the role book taking up the center of her desk. The rest of the stack of role books were piled up on the edge instead of being up on the shelf where they belonged. "You can go now," she added, sitting back in her chair and stretching her tired and cramped back.

When the king's guard had come back from the battlefields, she'd been hard pressed to find them things to do. There were too many of them, even if she doubled or tripled the guards in the palace, as well as the troops out at the edges of Trollville, patrolling for trouble.

Luckily, when the troops arrived, the first thing most of them did was apply for family leave. Ozlandia had granted it gladly, putting off the problem of what to do with them until they came back.

When they returned to the palace, generally just a day

or two later, they started resigning. In droves. "Family matters," was all the excuse most of them gave.

Ozlandia had been too swamped with striking all the names of the trolls from the role books, as well as keeping lists for the treasurer of all the pensions, to realize what was happening next.

The "retired" king's guard marched straight out of her office to the fairy bridge, where they gathered quietly in the human world before being sent straight back to war.

Ozlandia knew that Kizalynn hadn't put the guard up to it. She'd proposed the solution, certainly. However, the troops had taken it upon themselves to fully divest themselves from the king.

It seemed as though the trolls had, indeed, all gone back to their families. Retiring from the guard wasn't a decision they'd make on their own. Instead, they'd gotten their family's blessing to return to the war, going back to Kizalynn's side, rather than keep their allegiance to the king.

A quiet noise made Ozlandia look back up from her books. Cactimakus still stood there. He'd just cleared his throat.

"Yes?" Ozlandia said. "What is it?"

"Are we doing the right thing, here?" he asked.

"What do you mean?" Ozlandia said, not sure which part of the entire operation that he was referring to.

"Staying," he said.

Ozlandia took a deep, exasperated breath before she replied to the young troll. "I took an oath to the king, same as you, same as the rest of the troops," she said slowly. She'd certainly thought through her response before. It felt different, though, to actually be saying it out loud.

"I know that corrupted items have been discovered in the palace," she continued. "I know that trolls, good trolls, have been influenced by the demons. However, I can't conveniently forget my oath. The king has not been proven unworthy. The court has not convicted him of no longer being trustworthy."

Cactimakus didn't say anything. He did grimace loud enough for her to respond.

"I will not turn my back on him until he's been proven compromised," Ozlandia said sternly. "He's the king."

Cactimakus nodded. "I will stay with you," he said softly. "Good night."

Ozlandia shook her head but didn't call her assistant back. That was *exactly* the sort of thing that she'd been trying to avert, trolls making their allegiance to other trolls instead of to the king.

She knew, better than most, that sometimes leaders had to make unpopular decisions. A good troll needed to obey those orders, whether she was happy about them or not. That was how the guard was run. Had always been run.

Her treacherous brain whispered doubts at her, particularly late at night after yet another day of watching good trolls leave the guard.

Was she right in doing this? Had she misplaced her loyalty? Was she sticking to her post despite what was obvious to all?

Shouldn't she leave as well?

Ozlandia sighed and pushed herself up to standing.

She stepped around her desk to the other side and bowed to the north before she started doing the short form of the traditional troll fighting technique. Her muscles protested, as she hadn't been fighting but had been sitting all day, for the last several days.

Good solid dirt pushed up against her feet. The smell of her own sweat overtook the scent of dry books and ink. Light from the oil lamps in the corner threw odd shadows on the walls, nothing solid for her to fight. Ozlandia adjusted her form for the small room, only partially expanding a strike or blocking a kick.

By the time Ozlandia finished, she had her answer, though she didn't like it.

She was staying, despite how the king was probably corrupt, despite having her hands tied, despite operating in a space that grew smaller by the day.

Someone had to be here to do the work. That was as much a part of her duty as anything else.

And someone needed to be here to pick up the pieces of the kingdom when it all came crumbling apart.

CHAPTER TWENTY-FIVE

TINA GAVE A FRUSTRATED SIGH AS SHE KNOCKED OVER the entire tiny pile of sand in front of her.

"Again," Ty announced, standing like a foreboding god in the corner.

They were in a rented gym room on the human plane. Though Christine had told Tina about the gym she regularly went to north of Seattle in Shoreline, Tina had never gone there before. At least half the beings who went to the gym were *kith and kin*, and so the manager had been glad to rent them a well-contained room that could handle both magical as well as stronger-than-human physical attacks.

Mirrors completely covered one wall, while the others were made out of solid gray concrete. The wooden floor had a bounce to it, like a dance floor. A few kettlebells sat in one corner, while the back of the room had a pile of mats stacked up, along with a rack of hand weights. It smelled of floor wax and sweat—probably mainly from her as they'd been in here for over an hour.

Ty was a demon hunter by trade. After some practice, he was able to scent whenever Tina was letting too much of her darkness out at one time. They'd also gathered a few charms and spells (provided by Vern) should Tina need some extra help regaining herself, pushing the darkness back.

Tina sat on one of the black rubber mats in the middle of the room. She used her fingers to gather together the sand in front of her into a small pile, not much bigger than one of those candy kisses. The sand felt cold to her, grainy, as well as slightly damp. She pressed it together carefully to form a point at the top, as Ty had shown her.

The mirrors showed that she didn't look any different —still with blonde hair pulled back into a ponytail, blue eyes, a pink workout shirt and black yoga pants. Ty wore a plain white T-shirt that showed off all his wiry muscles, along with white karate pants, his long skinny feet sticking out from the bottoms of them.

But Tina sure felt different inside.

Ty had used an approach that Tina would never have thought of when it came to dealing with the dark magic inside of her. Instead of keeping it all bottled up, tamped down and unwelcome, Ty had encouraged her to live with the darkness. It was still contained—she saw it as a large glass ball filled with smoke that took up much of her internal space, surrounded by golden, bubbling magic.

His reasoning was that she had to acknowledge the darkness was there, all the time. It wasn't a once-in-a-while thing. She could count on it always being there, whether she wanted it to be or not.

His main lesson the first few days was that she must

learn how to trust herself, to believe that she could keep it contained.

Ty had helped with some spells to start with as she grew used to the idea that she was stronger than the powers within her.

Though it had felt as though months had passed, they'd only been training for about a week. Already, Tina had made great progress. She didn't need the dampening spells that Ty had ready for her. Instead, she'd grown strong enough to feel as though she could begin to trust herself.

Something her adoptive parents had never taught her. Nor any of the myriad shrinks.

Now, she just had to figure out how to let only a little of that power out at a time, to tame it. Sure, it was easy when she wanted to lay waste to something. Tearing the ground apart, burning it, destroying all that was in her path—she had that down pat.

Ty insisted that in order to be in full control, she needed to learn how to finesse things with all that strength. Or she'd lose herself again.

He'd admitted that his teachers had forced him to do the same exercise that he was making her do: to knock merely grains of sand from the tiny pile that still mocked her.

He'd shown her how he did it, his hand changing from human to beast, with black fur and long deadly talons emerging. With a flick of his claw, he removed the top portion of the sand pile. It took over a dozen small movements before he'd decimated it.

Then he'd challenged her to do the same.

Physically, Tina could easily do what he'd demonstrated.

Magically was a whole other beast.

Before Tina could start to focus again, Ty interrupted. "How are you holding the powers inside of you?"

"Glass bubble," Tina said, not looking up, her attention focused on the sand in front of her that determinedly would not just disappear grain by grain.

"For me, the wolf is just under my skin. It's like a second body, inside of me," Ty said slowly. "Do you need to let the darker powers expand? Or contain them differently?"

Huh. Tina hadn't thought of that. She'd chosen the glass so that she'd see the shadows and darkness. She knew intuitively that hiding it would be wrong.

But glass was impermeable. It could be broken or shattered. It separated materials. It didn't mix them.

Maybe she'd been going about this all wrong.

She'd always thought her own magic bubbled, like champagne or even tonic water. Fizzing and effervescent.

Could she instead form a bubble, not glass, but gas? Something that would allow the darkness to pass through when she wanted it to?

Tina closed her eyes and tried to reshape the glass ball. She thinned its walls, willing the nature of the glass change.

But she couldn't let the darkness out. It would engulf her, and Ty would have to call her back to herself again.

Bubbles, though, seemed to be the key. She brought up her own light, her golden magic, the pure, undiluted stream of her true self.

She'd always imagined the bubbles inside of her as small but irrepressible.

Should she just break the darkness into tiny pieces? Have the dark and the light mingle together freely? Streams of light and black bubbles?

That seemed like a quick road to full corruption again. No, the darkness needed to be more contained than that.

Could she grow one of her tiny bubbles to be the right size to contain the darkness?

She captured one in her head, gently using just her fingertips. It was such aa slight thing. One flick of her nail and it would be gone. It barely had any weight.

She imagined it growing larger. First, big enough to fill her hand. Then bigger than her own head. The skin of the bubble grew thicker in order to support its increased volume. Finally, it was the size of a large beachball, bigger than the glass bubble that contained the dark magic.

Slowly, carefully, Tina pressed the gas magical bubble up against the glass holding the shadows. The bubble of light was permeable, and so she could merge the two if she went slowly enough.

Finally, she had her darkest powers contained in both a glass sphere as well as a lighter, magical one. "Gonna try something," she warned Ty. If this didn't work, he might have to drag her back again.

Without looking, she knew that he'd transform himself halfway between human and wolf so he could catch her scent better.

Tina was scared to let the glass ball dissolve. It had taken her hours to figure out how to bring the darkness into herself and yet keep it contained.

That solution wasn't working, though. She needed to try something else.

After taking another deep breath, reminding herself that she had a physical body, Tina released the glass.

The darkness swelled immediately, pushing against the magical, golden bubble that she'd caught it in. Tina could hear her own gasp.

The golden light held. It contained the darkness and didn't let even a whiff of it escape.

Maintaining the gas bubble would take more work than the glass. However, Tina could tell that this was a much more natural solution for her. Bubbles had always kind of been her thing. Not glass balls.

Turning her attention back outward, Tina reached forward with just a sliver of power and knocked the first few grains of sand off the pile.

"Good," Ty said.

Tina smiled.

"Again," he commanded.

Tina bit her lips in frustration rather than yell at him. Couldn't she just revel in her victory for a few moments?

She looked inside. The golden bubble held. She could tell her darker side was pushing to get out. She could practically hear it laughing at her, challenging her.

Familiar dark thoughts rose up. Who was she to deny the demonic corruption that had so totally ruined her life? She stood no chance against it. She would always be vulnerable, always be just on the verge of giving in. Why didn't she just go the easy route and let it win?

Because that wasn't who she was.

Yes, through her entire life, everything had always

come effortlessly to her. Her magic had been unstoppable. She'd been raised privileged, the golden child with a great Destiny before her.

She didn't know if she still had a Destiny. It didn't matter.

She had herself now. Finally. A self that she could trust to turn away from the depression and the black magic, a self who would always seek the light.

A thought occurred to her, something that Christine had once talked about, how the fates or the Host or whoever had placed a troll in the Tuckermans had known what they were doing.

Christine had been raised that a Tuckerman always kept their word. It had turned out that trolls, too, were fanatical about their promises, particularly troll royalty.

Tina made herself a promise that she would *never* give into the dark side. She'd go out fighting.

The darkness inside of her paused for a moment, withdrawing from the inside of her golden bubble, no longer pressing against it and seeking a way out but instead, coalescing into a solid form.

Tina stood in front of it, hands ready to blast that black power into tiny pieces if it tried anything. She'd keep her word. The darkness would try, but it would never get the upper hand again permanently.

She swore a sacred oath to herself about that.

Someone softly called Tina's name. She blinked, realizing that she was still in the gym room with Ty, though her physical body was now standing as well.

"Just a moment," Tina said, returning her attention inside.

The golden bubble looked different now. It glowed with its own light, shielding her from the darkness, like a moon during a full eclipse of the sun.

With the tiniest of efforts, Tina siphoned off a stream of smoke, sending it out into the gym room, knocking off just three more grains of sand from the pile sitting between her feet.

When she opened her eyes, she couldn't help but laugh at Ty's startled expression.

"I can trust myself," she said clearly, possibly for the first time in her life. "I will do the right thing."

Ty gave her a broad smile in return. "Good," he said. "You will have to keep training," he added, peering at her.

"I know," Tina said. It was like suddenly discovering she was a secret alcoholic. Just because she'd kicked the beast to the curb that day didn't mean it wouldn't come haunting her dreams or her down times.

"I will keep up my training," Tina promised, both to herself as well as Ty. "Do the meditations you've taught me. Keep reaching for the light."

"Huh," Ty said. He didn't bother hiding how he scented the air. "Your scent changed suddenly," he said as his features melted back to fully human. "You're not corrupted, I can't scent demon on you. But the smell changed." He shrugged. "Deeper, no longer so light, though still you."

"Not as much like an airheaded girl?" Tina guessed.

"No comment," Ty said wisely.

Tina gave him a huge grin. "Thank you," she said. "I wouldn't be here without you."

"We should still keep meeting," Ty said. They quickly

arranged a once a week check in, at least for a few months, like a sponsor. And Ty assured her that she could call him anytime she needed to talk with someone, day or night.

"What are you going to do next?" Ty asked as they both got ready to go.

"I have some cleaning to do."

CHAPTER TWENTY-SIX

Buddy fussed with the centerpiece his minion had created. It wasn't quite right. The golden sword stood up straight and tall from the center of the piece, with chunks of ice and fire falling from it in a beautiful display of power. It smelled of strength and brimstone, and was certain to be the envy of all the demons viewing it.

It had taken three long, tiresome meetings with Lars before Buddy had finally agreed that the best theme for the party was the golden age.

After all, wasn't that the prospect awaiting them?

The large hall where the party would occur was finally taking shape. The number of tables had been approved, then reapproved, then finally settled on for the last time. Then the chairs had to be counted and recounted, moved around to give more standing room, more sitting room, and so on. Each change had required Lars' signature.

Golden streamers hung from the thick rock overhead, while glitter had been liberally applied to the stone walls. Buddy knew from experience that even a powerful demon couldn't just dismiss glitter once they had been infected with it.

No, glitter removal was a process that most demons wouldn't bother with, and they'd just be tortured by it forever.

Buddy returned his attention to the grand centerpiece. Lars would probably be able to approve it as it was, right away.

And Buddy couldn't have that. So he pushed on the sword until it was slightly off center.

That had been one of the interesting things Buddy had learned about Lars, that he had almost human level OCD when it came to these sorts of details. It was what had made him such a good leader for the Great War, his attention to detail.

It would be Lars' downfall, that human nature. Buddy would see to that.

His own plan was working beautifully. Lars' attention, every time he returned to hell, was fully focused where Buddy had intended, on his own party. Which left Buddy time and opportunity to bring the other princes of hell back into the fold, focused on their own interests or agreeing with Buddy that Lars in charge would be a bad idea.

That Lars now appeared to be losing the Great War just helped Buddy's cause.

Was Buddy causing Lars to lose the Great War? No, no one (except Lars) could accuse Buddy of that. Lars could always put his foot down. Instead of this grand ball, he could insist on a taco truck and an unending supply of beer. Maybe a death-metal llama band. The Host might even show up for something like that and make it a truly memorable event. *That* would be Buddy's idea of a party.

Lars, and his ego, would never settle for something so simple. So it really was his own damned fault.

Buddy took a picture of the centerpiece and attached a note, "Something not quite right. What do you think?" Then he sent the text to Lars, making sure that it would ping his device in the middle of something important, like during a meeting with his generals, during a meal, or even while he was sleeping.

Lars hadn't learned that trick either. He was so focused on grand gestures that he forgot (or never bothered learning) the fine art of torturing a being with little things.

Yes, there was much that the young demon didn't know.

One of the things that Buddy had learned from Lars was the ability to make contingency plans. Who would have thought of such a thing? They still made Buddy's head hurt when he tried.

However, Buddy had learned the lesson well. If Lars did win the Great War, Buddy still had Curly waiting in the wings, armed with a blade that would suck Lars' soul out at the most inopportune moment.

No matter what, Buddy would end up on top. And really, wasn't that what mattered most?

CHAPTER TWENTY-SEVEN

Christine's jubilation over her most recent wins died the moment she stepped into the throne room and saw the king.

The trolls in the court, at least, still wore a mixture of good jewel-toned colors and metallics. She couldn't tell by looking at them whether they'd been corrupted or if they were reflecting what was before them.

King Garethen, on the other hand, was no longer in his beautiful reds or greens. Instead, he wore a silver vest with little decoration embroidered into the cloth, the color of the material unbroken. She would bet that he had similar ones done in black and gold, possibly brown as well.

He looked so similar to how she'd first seen him, sitting alone and hunched over on his throne, with long white hair weighed down with a gold crown and gold rings on all his fingers. His tusks had yellowed further with age and looked more brittle than ever.

"Ah! Niece!" the king said, faking a heartiness that

Christine could hear. "What news do you bring us of the war?"

Christine didn't want to put on a show. Still, she knew that she must. She had to keep the court on her side, at least those who hadn't been corrupted.

"The news is good, my liege," Christine said. She pulled herself upright and looked out over the trolls standing there. She felt herself slip into "princess" mode, pulling out of her usual librarian self.

Not a prissy princess though, not one who simpered and demanded that all things go her way.

No, as Dennis had labeled her, she was *badass warrior princess*, used to command and being obeyed.

"It started with the complete route of the demons when they came back to attack the world of the rowdy boys, the Risilodan," she explained. "We finally took the field, not only pushing back the invasion, but then following the demons to their staging area and wiping most of them out." She paused, drawing more eyes to her. "That win was only possible because of the large number of free-fighting trolls."

Then Christine turned and addressed the king again. "Since then, every battle has been either a decisive win, or come to a draw, with the demons calling the retreat first. They've been sending their left overs at us, weaker demons. They're afraid to send their stronger troops because those, too, will fail."

After a polite cheer, Christine went on. Most of the court appeared to be fully engaged. That meant fewer had been corrupted than what they wore would indicate.

"There will be one great, deciding battle," she said.

"These little victories, while important, mean nothing. We have to get at the head of the serpent and kill their Supreme General. Once I do that, the war will be over."

"Is that possible?" the king asked, doubt shading his tone.

Christine gave a mirthless laugh. "Not only possible, sire, but inevitable." She knew she was bragging slightly. Lars could always pull a trick that would surprise her and put her at a disadvantage. She just had to hold onto the winning edge for a short while longer. Though it felt to her as though the push had gone on forever, she just had to endure for a few more weeks at most.

The rest of the court cheered at her proclamation, a loud roar that built up until it pulsed through Christine's chest.

That was the proper response, even from the court who considered themselves too refined for such a reaction. It warmed Christine's heart, even as the king ended the cheering too soon.

"I would speak with my heir, alone," he announced, sending the rest of the court on their way.

More than one of the properly dressed trolls came up and congratulated Christine on their way out of the throne room. Christine noted them as well, keeping lists of allies as well as potential enemies.

"Well done, niece, well done," King Garethen said heartily as the last of the court left the room.

"Thank you," Christine said. She found herself taking a wider fighting stance, as if facing a great battle.

She purposefully kept the lights in the throne room bright, sending a trickle of magic to the beautiful gems located *in situ* on the walls and ceiling. The smell of the court remained, too sweet for her tastes, though she knew that some trolls liked perfume. Good solid rock pushed up against her feet, giving her a steady base on which to stand.

The king slowly rose from his throne and stepped off the dais to face her. After a moment, he held out his hands so that they might clasp arms like soldiers.

"I do mean it," the king said, holding her arms in a tight grip. "I am happy for your wins. But in the face of that, we need to start looking toward the future."

Christine merely nodded, letting go of the king's arms. She refused to step away or back. If he wanted to confront her, it had to be on her terms, not his.

The king didn't test her, however. Instead, he was the one who took a step back, then started pacing across the floor of the throne room.

"In order to continue our family's rule, you are going to have to get married, and soon. Then, you'll need to produce an heir," he instructed her.

Christine felt her head spin. She hadn't expected this. She hadn't even won the war yet! She wasn't ready to have to suddenly settle down and start popping out babies.

She was pretty sure she didn't like kids. Though that may have been a leftover artifact from the changeling spell, as Tina was mightily opposed to ever raising children. Christine realized that she actually had no idea how she felt about children, never having been around any.

"Honestly? I've never thought about marriage," Christine said. She'd had a few boyfriends, always trolls, but no one who she'd ever wanted to spend the rest of her life with. Rule with. Raise kids with.

"You need to start thinking about it now," the king said.

Christine didn't even know how to reply to that. She opened her mouth, but no words came out.

The king gave her a kind chuckle. "It's all right. I understand that the topic is overwhelming, at first. Good thing I have been giving it some thought. I might even have a candidate for you to consider."

"Really?" Christine asked. "Who?" Who had the king been consorting with? He hadn't done anything so stupid as tried to arrange something for her behind her back, had he? Was this part of the demonic influence? Or was he really thinking about what was best for the kingdom?

Most troll royalty did have semi-arranged marriages—the matches made both because it was good political sense as well as because the trolls figured they could come to love each other.

"He's a fine young troll, from a good family," King Garethen assured her. "And he's spent time on the human plane as well, several years, in fact, so he's comfortable there."

"That sounds good," Christine said. In fact, that was exactly the sort of thing she'd be looking for in a mate, someone who could easily travel to the human plane with her.

She wasn't about to give up her human family. She could easily imagine the glee her mother might express about having grandkids. Even if they were troll babies.

"You think you might agree to such a match?" the king asked.

Christine didn't like the gleam in his eyes. "What's his name?" she asked warily.

"Josekanly Zelelinna D'Angelino," the king said triumphantly.

"I don't know who that is," Christine said slowly. "I don't think I've met him."

"But you have!" the king said. "Back on the human plane."

Christine thought furiously for a moment. What trolls had she met there? There hadn't been many. Trolls tended not to go to the human plane.

"Josekanly…Joe…wait a minute, you don't mean Joe D'Angelo?" Christine asked, appalled. Her old boyfriend, Joe the marketing troll? "He's got royal blood?" she said, remembering how he'd been so appalled by her magic.

"He does," the king said proudly.

"He has no magic," Christine said after a moment. "None. Said he'd been teased about it as a child." Now, she was putting it all together. No troll child would have been upset about not having magic.

Not unless they were royalty and supposed to have it. Most trolls had none.

"You have more than enough magic for the pair of you," the king said airily. He stopped his pacing and turned to her, with a huge smile on his face. "So you agree?"

"Hell no," Christine said. "Did he tell you that he destroyed the fairy bridge? The first one I built?"

"He did, as a matter of fact," the king said smugly.

"Said he was saving you from yourself, from showing the world such sloppy work. As a troll, he was ashamed of what you'd built."

Christine sighed. What Joe claimed was a partial truth. That first attempt of hers had been flawed. But he hadn't done it with such clear intentions.

"You know who prompted him to tear the bridge apart? It wasn't his own higher nature," Christine said. "Joe had been hired by Lars to tear it down. You know. Lars Sorgenfreys. The demon leading the armies in the Great War?"

"What?" the king asked, obviously shocked.

"Joe was working for Lars at the time," Christine said, gentling her tone. "It's all in the court records, kept by the Host. He received a huge fine for doing it, though he didn't go to jail." She'd followed what had happened to him out of guilt. "I would bet that Lars paid off the rest of his bond. Or some demon did. Which left Joe free to come back here and spread his corruption."

"Are you sure?" the king asked. He suddenly looked older than he had, lines carved deeper into his face, the healthy green color now tinged with gray.

"Here," Christine said abruptly. She held out her hand. The king took it, a slight tremor echoing through his body. He let her meekly lead him back up to the throne where he sat.

Christine's air and water powers fetched him a long cool draught of water, which the king gulped down.

Truly, he hadn't been expecting this news at all.

After the king had thanked Christine for the water, she

knelt down next to the throne so that they were closer to eye level.

"Uncle—you've been fooled," Christine said softly. "Again."

"I know, I know," King Garethen said, shaking his head. "He seemed like such an honest young troll! Maybe he paid off his debt himself?"

"No, uncle," Christine said. "He took money from demons. He has in the past and will again in the future. Uncle…your judgment in this isn't sound."

Christine knew she was walking on thin ice for even making the suggestion that the king was compromised.

The king looked as if he wanted to argue. She could tell he had blustering, blistering arguments all lined up.

Instead, Christine reached out and placed her hand on his arm. She called her air power to bring in bright, cool winds from the mountains, her fire elemental to warm the king's feet.

The king took a deep breath. "I will cut all ties to Josekanly and his family," the king promised.

That might be going too far—Christine didn't know how far the corruption had spread—but it wasn't an argument for here and now. The king had always been all about going to extremes.

"You know that while parts of the palace have been cleaned from demonic influence, parts haven't been," she said, trying not to rouse his anger or his greed.

"I know," he said. "And thank you for that," he said absentmindedly.

Christine knew he didn't mean it. Removing the demonic influence had probably made the king more irritable, as it had removed all the soothing corruption he'd been experiencing. That was probably part of the reason why the king had liked Josekanly so much, because the troll was corrupted through and through.

"Your judgment hasn't been sound for a while now," Christine said gently.

"I suppose you want me to step down," the king said, his tone harsh again. "Abdicate the throne. Turn it over to you."

"Yes," Christine said, glad that he'd brought it up first. "Not right away," she added quickly, trying to reassure him. "We need to wait until the war is actually over. But yes, you need to step down, Uncle. I will promise to find a suitable mate, one you can approve of. And…" Christine paused, gulped, then made herself continue, "I'll provide heirs at some point as well."

She hadn't actually made the promise. Just said that she would when the time came.

She'd been fighting the Great War. Surely raising kids would be easy in comparison.

"I will think on what you've said," the king said.

"You promise you will think about it?" Christine said, digging in. She'd heard him use that phrase before, generally to dismiss someone he disagreed with.

The king paused. "I promise to consider giving abdicating serious thought," he said eventually.

"Abdicating in the near future, not some distant one," Christine insisted.

Nodding, the king said, "Yes. Stepping down soon after the war is over. I had thought about it before, you know," he said. Then he gave her a true smile.

"Particularly since there may be grandchildren coming my way."

It was Christine's turn to gulp. She'd been aware that finding a mate and having offspring had always been in her future, particularly once she'd discovered that she was royalty, doubly so when the king officially made her his heir.

Seemed that faraway someday was rapidly approaching.

"Goodbye, Uncle," Christine said. On impulse, she leaned forward and kissed his cheek, just to make him smile once more.

Then Christine put back on her *badass warrior princess* mask and headed back out the door.

Time to win this war once and for all.

CHAPTER TWENTY-EIGHT

TINA SHUDDERED WHEN SHE POPPED BACK INTO HER old practice room.

The rot had spread again, possibly further than it had been before. Black spots of corruption spread like mold across the bottom of all the walls. It was as if the room had been underwater while she'd been gone, emptying only when she came back. The smell of rotting drywall mingled with the scent of filth. The pads on the floor felt soggy.

Should she just give up on this place? Was it worth the work to clean it?

Tina still didn't have a good answer to that. She could only try.

Slowly, Tina siphoned off a thin trail of dark magic, mingling it with her own light, then directing it toward the first wall.

It appeared that the demons hadn't returned and placed more of the corruption crystals along the base of all the walls, as she'd first thought. The first wall was cleaned up quickly. She bleached the color as she worked, changing the beautiful green to be a sterile white. The smell of decay faded as she worked. The pads under her feet firmed up, providing comfortable support again.

The next two walls also cleaned up quickly. A few corruption crystals had remained along the base of those walls, outside in the non-space that she'd carved the room from.

Tina couldn't help but gasp as she reached the far wall.

The demons had doubled down on heaping up corruption crystals there. The pile stood twice as high now, maybe as tall as her, nearly five feet up. Crystals lined the edges of the wall on either side of the great mound, as much as three inches thick in places.

Tina took a deep breath. She was going to need more power to clean this.

Slowly, carefully, Tina siphoned off more of the dark magic from the gas bubble inside of her, focusing the stream of absolute power through and out her hands.

She hadn't bothered with a wand this time. Wands, she'd discovered, were for focused work, like knocking grains of sand from a pile.

She needed to use her hands and get dirty when she wanted to do the big stuff.

She lifted her hands up, palms out, facing the wall.

The pile of corruption crystals mocked her. So many had been gathered there that the malevolence had a rudimentary awareness to it. It had laughed at her feeble efforts to control it before.

Tina *blasted* the wall, setting it blazing with white hot magic, burning out the corruption on the other side.

At first, it appeared to be working. The pile melted into itself, the hard rocks turning into sludge.

However, when Tina finished, she realized her mistake.

The individual crystals had coalesced into a solid mass, making it much more difficult to just sweep away than the smaller rocks. It had a sticky quality to it as well. She knew if she ever touched it physically, she'd never be able to wipe away it from her skin and to ever feel clean again.

Could she just blast it? No, that wouldn't work. It would take more power than even she could tap into.

She stood in the middle of the room, her head bent in sorrow. This had been her safe space. Her practice room. The one spot where she delighted in her magic. Coming here had always made her heart sing.

She was going to have to give it up, though. Discard it and build herself a new practice room.

Tina turned away and headed toward the wall where she always opened up a portal.

Then a different thought occurred to her.

Why the hell not?

Tina turned back and walked to the wall closest to the remaining sludge of corruption. It reached for her, a thousand tendrils of corruption, wanting to control her, to cover her in filth.

To make her doubt herself again.

Tina physically put her foot down.

She would *not* go back down that path again. Not ever.

She could trust herself, regardless of who else did or didn't.

After taking a deep breath and calming herself for a

moment, Tina reached out with the tiniest tendril of mixed power, the black magic well mixed with the light.

Then she flicked away the smallest piece of corruption from the edge of the pool outside the wall, dispersing just a single drop.

The slag laughed at her puny efforts.

Tina split her single stream into two, each of the thin shoots cleaning off tiny drops.

She ignored the doubts that the darkness tried to raise, ignored her own thoughts about how long this was going to take as she split her power again and again. She ended up with hundreds of flickers of magic, each taking the smallest piece imaginable from the larger pile and annihilating it.

The corruption crystals worked slowly, accumulatively. Why couldn't she do the same when it came to destroying them? Just a few grains at a time.

Tina felt when the rudimentary awareness finally acknowledged that it might have been mistaken—its own demise was on the horizon. She laughed now at its cursing as it disappeared along with the rest of its mass.

How long did it take? Tina was never certain. It was more than hours, but possibly less than days, before she finally dispersed the last of the filth accumulated outside the walls of her practice room.

Tina came back to her physical presence and blinked, surprised. The walls were pure white now. She hated that color. Her adoptive parents lived in black and white. That was what they'd taught her growing up.

While Tina—Tina now lived somewhere in between.

She colored the walls a light blue-gray. The light for

the room came from a couple of magical spots she'd designated on the ceiling. Changing the amount of brightness transformed the walls from almost white to a darker, angry sea color.

Tina had no doubt that the next time she returned to her practice room that the stupid demons would have placed more of the corruption crystals along the bases of the walls again.

It would be good practice for her to use the finessing part of her magic to clean them up every time.

She looked around her practice room one last time, glad she'd put in the effort to reclaim it, content with her ongoing work.

Now, she had one last thing to clean up.

***

"What do you mean, I can trust you now?" Christine asked, looking both alarmed as well as confused.

Tina sighed. This wasn't going as well as she'd hoped. She'd gotten Christine to agree to meet her at their favorite coffee shop, the one that didn't play loud music and had comfy chairs at the back. They both wore soft sweaters—Christine's in a beautiful fall red, while Tina continued to wear more grays. They also appeared as sisters physically, just with different coloring.

"You couldn't trust me before," Tina admitted, taking a sip of her most excellent mocha. "I know that."

Christine nodded slowly. She pressed her lips together before she finally said, "Never trust a human."

Tina swallowed down her exclamation. Did Christine really believe that?

"Nik told me that," Christine admitted. "They're too easily influenced by demons."

Tina nodded, understanding. Christine had told her about Nik, how he'd once been human and had transferred his consciousness to his little wooden body in order to avoid demonic influence.

"I have been influenced by demons, more than once," Tina repeated.

Christine merely nodded. She'd been on the receiving end of Tina's influence, more than once.

"But I won't be again," Tina added. "You can trust me."

"How?" Christine asked flatly, clearly not believing Tina's statement.

Tina sighed, trying to figure out (again!) how to put what she knew into words that Christine would understand.

"I have both light and dark powers inside of me," Tina said. "My adoptive parents, and most of the human magical community, would have me ignore the black magic. Put it into a box and shove it into the closet."

"Okay?" Christine said, following along.

"Being in the closet has never really worked for me," Tina said with a shy smile. It was why she'd lost her last girlfriend, because she hadn't been as out and proud. Well, that, and the demonic possession.

"True," Christine agreed, also smiling.

"I need to face that darkness. Acknowledge it. Live with it. Choose how I let it express itself. With gold bubbles, and maybe glitter," Tina said, grinning. "Not let it have its head."

Christine peered at her closely. "Go on," she said.

Tina didn't roll her eyes at how Christine was trying to be subtle about how she sniffed at Tina, trying to pick up her scent.

"I'm *not* corrupted," Tina assured her. "Ask Ty." They'd met for lunch earlier that day. Ty had been impressed with how integrated Tina had become.

Christine nodded and admitted, "I did. He said you've made great progress."

"I have," Tina said. She shook her head. "When I think about where I was, even a week ago…I know I've come a long way." She turned in her seat to directly face Christine. "I can trust myself now."

"Hmmm," was all the response she got.

"Okay, so before, I never even thought about what it meant to trust myself," Tina said earnestly. "Now, I meditate and practice, every day, so that I know, deep in my bones, that I can trust myself and my power. The demons will always try to influence me. I know how to sense it, now, and keep it at bay."

"What does this mean?" Christina asked. "For us?"

Tina took a deep breath, then let it out. "My Destiny has always been tied up with yours," she said quietly. "And with the Great War. I think we both need to be there during the final battle."

Christine sat back in her chair and sipped at her tea while she thought.

Tina wanted to fidget and squirm, to try to say something, anything, to get Christine to agree.

She knew she was right. She knew that the demons would never be able to take over her consciousness again. They would try. They would fail.

Finally, Christine nodded. "I would welcome your help," she said softly. "But my trust…that's going to take a while. You're going to have to earn it. As long as I can contain you, you may come and fight with me."

"Thank you," Tina said. "And thank you for being honest with me, for not lying about trusting me."

She paused, then reached out her hand. "I'd like to be friends again. True friends."

Christine reached out and squeezed her fingers gently. "While a part of me longs for that as well, I don't want to go back. Even though what we had was good, I want us to keep moving forward."

"Ditto," Tina said, letting go of Christine's very hot hand. "We need to come up with new things to do."

"When the war is over," Christine warned.

"Here's to it ending soon," Tina said, raising her mug in a salute.

She'd fought her own private war. And won. Now she could finally help end the other as well.

CHAPTER TWENTY-NINE

Really, trolls should never try to be subtle. Lars couldn't help but roll his eyes at the outright summons that Christine had issued while thinking that she was being tricky.

Trolls didn't understand sly. Even a troll who'd been raised as a human and had proven herself kind of sneaky.

Lars sat in his command center on the human plane, considering the report he'd just been handed. He hadn't updated any of the maps covering the walls—really, all those bloody spots that had at one point been demon victories would change hands again. He didn't need for those maps to be accurate. He would make damned sure that they were correct later, after he'd won the Great War.

He could still win. But he had to cut the head from his enemy. Christine had rallied her trolls in greater numbers than he'd ever imagined or even planned for. Never had he suspected that inciting infighting among the troll court would end up in the common troll siding with Christine, allying themselves away from the king.

And Joe the troll had been sent away from the palace. Lars still had plans for him, just different plans than what he'd started with.

The king of the trolls himself had to be Lars' focus now.

And Lars knew how to defeat him.

Kill Christine.

That empty spot just behind him would be filled with her head soon.

Christine had been secretly gathering her troops together. Well, at least she'd *thought* she was being secretive. She didn't realize how many demons were following her troop movements.

She'd set her sights on the world of the Conethiquans as the final battlefield. Her minions had already divested the plane of the demons who had been there, scouting. Lars had her intelligence report right there, as well as the plan to challenge him directly, once the trolls had taken the field there.

The world itself was a nightmare for most demons. Planes of ice, snow-covered mountains, that sort of thing. His troops really would be at a disadvantage there.

Lars snorted. Christine was such a child when it came to these sorts of things! She had no idea how to actually *plan*.

His phone pinged as he started arranging his troops, the interruption seriously annoying.

He glanced at his phone and chose to ignore the latest text from Buddy. (Though how Buddy managed to make such a human thing as text messaging work from the depths of hell was a trick Lars had yet to figure out.) The damned party could wait until Lars actually went ahead and won the Great War.

Christine would never expect Lars and his armies to just show up on the plane she'd been using for staging her massive attack. It wasn't the ideal spot—just a barren world filled with rocks and a couple oceans. But it was sure better than those awful ice fields.

Time to go and prove her wrong, and to end this war once and for all.

LARS LAUGHED TRIUMPHANTLY AS HE APPROACHED the field of battle.

He was a big enough demon to admit that he had been worried. At least for a few moments.

For the first time, Christine didn't stand alone amongst her warriors. Another stood beside her, armed with a sword and shield, wearing a black ringed vest instead of the dark blue favored by the trolls.

It took Lars a moment to recognize Tina, Christine's human doppelganger.

He laughed again. Tina was so easily influenced! Surely this was a huge mistake on Christine's part. All he had to do was to focus on Tina, get her to turn on the "sister" standing beside her.

They were doing his work for him. Going to make this easy for him. Idiots.

He could already taste the steady stream of congratulations and honors about to be bestowed on him, how sweet and hot they'd flow, like a stream of the finest blood.

He ignored Christine, absentmindedly defending himself from her first fumbled blow while he focused all his attention on Tina. He crowed out loud when he felt his influence easily slip behind the shield that Tina had foolishly thought would block him out.

Fool.

But then Tina took all that power focused on her and directed it back at him. The lightning bolt she directed with her sword caused him to fly backwards several feet.

What the hell!!??!?!?!

"Begone, worm," Tina said, laughing at him. Laughing at him!

The sound of human laughter still set his already acid blood to boiling hotter.

It wasn't possible for her to use his own attack against him like that. He'd never even *heard* of such a thing!

No matter. He would ignore the human and focus his attack on Christine, as he should have been doing all along. He could deal with the stupid human later.

He jumped and landed in front of the pair of them, towering over them. They were fools not to cower before his magnificence. "It is time for the pair of you to die," he proclaimed, sure that if he came up with a snappier line later that he'd be able to edit the history books.

It was kind of amazing how Tina and Christine had synchronized their eye roll.

"You will never win," Christine said, stepping forward and taking a swipe at him with her great ax.

Lars had studied recordings of how Christine

physically fought. He had it down to a dance, a well-choreographed set of steps. First she'd slash, then she'd pivot and kick out with a well-placed foot, followed immediately by another swipe of her blade.

He easily avoided all her moves and readied himself to go on the offensive, to slice at her with his own huge fiery sword.

He had *not* expected the blow from Tina that suddenly knocked him off balance, causing him to spin around, out of reach.

Christine closed quickly, keeping him on the defensive, backing away from her massive blade.

Only to slam his back hard against a wall of stone, placed there by Christine? Tina? Did it matter?

Lars roared out with more surprise than pain, spitting acid at the pair of them to keep them back.

Christine just smacked the side of his own personal shield with a barrage of rocks, while Tina slid fire up next to his toes, threatening to burn them off.

This was Not Good. Not Good at all.

Lars could defeat Christine. He had all sorts of moves planned that had been certain to defeat her.

He'd never imagined that she wouldn't be fighting on her own. That somehow, Tina would not only be free of her demonic influence, but be able to use it against those trying to control her.

He had no plan for this. No contingencies to cover this.

If he stayed, the outcome was inevitable.

Instead of Christine's head on his wall, she'd have his head on hers.

That was unacceptable.

Lars didn't bother sounding the general retreat. Let the armies fight it out. Sure, his side would lose a lot of good demons, but once they realized they were cornered, they'd fight harder. Dirtier. Meaner. He'd bleed Christine's army white before the rest of his demons called it quits.

Instead, Lars called up the spell he'd always labeled in his head as "Armageddon." He didn't think he'd ever be in this position, that he'd ever have to use it.

And he simply vanished.

LARS ANGRILY PACED ON THE BARREN WORLD HE'D returned to, the one he'd chosen after the battle with the obelisk of truth. He didn't know how Tina had managed to overcome her conditioning. No human had ever been able to withstand such direct influence before. Particularly not a human who had been corrupted more than once.

How had she done it? Could all humans now do this? What did it mean in terms of the Great War?

Lars had had to stop using the corruption crystals as the demons didn't trust them. Were the crystals still effective against the humans? Or had Tina and the others somehow found a way to deflect their influence as well?

Damn it! Lars needed more time. He was still alive, though. He could win the Great War, given time.

He just needed to figure out how. He needed better intelligence as well.

When he felt a presence impinging on his awareness, he eagerly let the demon join him. Whoever it was could be made to do Lars' bidding. Could find out what and how the humans had learned to deflect corruption.

It surprised him that Curly was the one who approached him. She had her spiked wings with red feathers stretched out, as if preparing for a demonic hug. Her glowing golden eyes held nothing but sympathy for her general. She kept her tail straight back, the spikes at the ready, as if preparing to defend herself from any fool who thought they could sneak up on her.

"What is it?" Lars asked, bracing himself for the grating, chalk-board scratching tone of her voice.

Except it didn't come.

Instead came a melodious croon, deep and soothing. "I came to see what I could do for you, my supreme commander," she said.

Lars blinked, surprised. "What happened to your voice?"

Demons did not blush. The polluted white scales of her face did darken a touch, though. "Someone pointed out to me that perhaps I would get further along in the army and achieve a higher rank if I spent some time perfecting my tones. Do you like it?"

Lars found himself nodding like a fool. "I do," he said, clearing his throat.

Damn it! This was not a good time for his libido to suddenly start acting up. He needed to think with the big head, not the little one.

"Is there anything I can do? Anything at all?" Curly said, her eyes gleaming as she stepped closer. "I'd be happy to serve you in your time of need."

Lars shivered as all sorts of lewd suggestions about what exactly she could do rose up in his imagination.

Curly took another step closer. "You just need to take it easy for a bit," she said. "Give that big brain of yours a rest."

Lars was *not* the type to be seduced. He'd always done the seducing. But he found himself leaning forward slightly, as if drawn into Curly's web.

"I could help," she suggested throatily, her voice like sex itself. "Reward you as you deserve, let your subconscious come up with the next great plan while you recover."

That actually did sound like a grand idea. He knew that humans did their best "thinking" when they were half-conscious. He'd never tried it before.

Surely it wouldn't hurt?

"I've always admired you," Curly said, her icy breath sending chills across his shoulders as she drew closer. "Have always wanted to learn more about you. Be closer to you."

"Have you now?" Lars said. He knew that his demon form didn't really smile, but he still felt one stretching across his features. "Then let's take care of that, shall we?"

He fell into her hot embrace, mashing their bodies together in ways that were impossible for humans.

He quickly fell into the rhythm surest to take him to a quick completion, Curly's body matching his intensity, prolonging his pleasure.

Almost there. Almost there…

Lars was so involved with seeking his own climax that

he never saw the knife. Only felt it enter him just before that crucial time, denying him completion.

He screamed and thrashed, but it was too late.

The blade sucked his soul away into itself, leaving him forever frustrated.

CHAPTER THIRTY

What the hell just happened?

Christine pulled back mid-swing.

Where had Lars gone?

She cast her air power out, seeking him. Was he still there? Had he just gone invisible?

But her winds came back empty handed.

Lars had left the field of battle.

Frustrated, Christine turned to Tina. "I can't find him," she growled.

Tina nodded. "I can't either. I think he's left this world. Some spell he must have used," she added, pointing to the scorched earth that had been under his feet. "A contained portal like that must have cost him a bunch of power. Might even have injured him."

Christine ground her teeth. "We have to find him. Stop him. Before he figures out how to survive and attack with both of us."

"Should I bring Ty in?" Tina asked.

"Good thought," Christine said. She signaled to her

closest general. "Sound the news. The Supreme General has been forced from the field."

Callers started shouting the news, Christine's wind power aiding their voices.

As soon as the demons heard that Lars had just vanished, they called their own retreat. Christine's troops followed them when they could, slaughtering them.

Christine helped with the route, Tina at her side. They fought really well together, though Christine could see that they'd need to start training together.

But she'd been impressed with how Tina handled herself in front of Lars. He'd sent a stream of influence so thick that Christine could practically smell it.

And Tina had done what she said she could—took it and used it against him.

The battle ended quickly, much more quickly than anyone had planned. At least Lars had originally taken the bait, and shown up on the "staging" plane. Christine and her generals had never planned on going anywhere else.

Now, Christine and her generals were going to have to figure out the next plan, see if they could trick Lars again into attacking.

Either that, or maybe she and Tina could somehow sneak into Lars' parent's house. She was still certain that was where he was staying, though she couldn't prove it.

After the battle, Christine found she wasn't completely exhausted. There hadn't been as much fighting and she found herself dissatisfied. It worried her sometimes how much she'd come to enjoy battling. And killing.

Still, she'd come up with a routine after every fight and she still followed it when she could. Since the demons had all left so abruptly, there was no reason for the troops to stay where they'd been gathered. She helped the various *kith and kin* races back to their home worlds, the ones who needed it. Then she slipped away herself, back to her underground home in the human plane, next to the fairy bridge.

The cambions hadn't been able to come over in such numbers once she set her mind against them. They still came in ones and twos, no longer carrying demons. She couldn't cut them off, not completely, not when the king had made a promise to them.

Christine spent a little bit of time in what she considered her backyard, breathing in the fresh fall winds of the Arboretum, enjoying the beautiful golds and reds of the trees, along with the soft misting rain.

This was what she'd been fighting for. To preserve this. She reminded herself every time she left a battle or whenever she felt discouraged.

Then Christine went into her home and straight to her tub, filling it with fizzing water and salts, willing her aching muscles to relax, her brain to unwind.

She couldn't stop the plans though. Where to meet Lars next. How to defeat him. She couldn't think about the future beyond that, about looking for a mate or maybe…kids.

It didn't take much for Christine to fall asleep that night, despite how wound up she still felt. Maybe it was the sound of the rain she could sense, just over her head, soothing her cares away.

In the morning, Christine woke up tense. She sprang out of her bed, calling her ax to her hand immediately.

Sure, most mornings that was overkill.

A little paranoia never hurt.

Christine growled when she saw the square white envelop sitting in the middle of what she considered her entranceway. It wasn't as if there was an actual tunnel that led from aboveground to her rooms. Still, this was where she brought in visitors, instead of dumping them directly into her living room.

Something had been here. Or had somehow managed to slip a message in past her defenses.

Christine poked at the envelop first with her magic, then with the handle of her ax.

Nothing demonic about it. Not a trap. The thing still turned her stomach and made her uneasy.

She finally realized that was because it had come from the Host.

Damn it! It wasn't some sort of summons, was it?

Christine finally put her ax away and picked up the envelop cautiously, trying to handle it just with her claws and not let the paper touch her skin.

The back had been sealed with red wax, then stamped with what looked like a bugle.

Huh.

Christine sliced the top of the envelop with her claws, pulling out the card within.

The body of Lars Sorgenfreys has been discovered on an abandoned world.

That was all the note said.

Christine turned it over, looking for more.

Then she read the message again.

The feel of the paper told Christine that the message was real. This was from the Host.

The Great War was over.

That couldn't be right. There had to be some mistake. She had to keep fighting. It was all she knew how to do.

How dare he just up and die like that? It had been *her* place to kill him, should have been *her* ax imbedded in his stupid skull. It wouldn't make up for all the lives that had been lost during the stupid war, but it would have been a good start.

Maybe she could keep fighting. There were other demons she could fight. Maybe she could get one of them to step up into Lars' position. Get them to continue the war so she could definitively win it, not just have this stupid sort of default position.

No, that was stupid. She should be glad that Lars was dead.

She sighed, her shoulders slumping.

Christine had never been sure what she'd do once she'd killed Lars. She'd thought that maybe she'd crow and dance. Perhaps even cry, or shout in triumph.

She didn't expect to feel empty.

Lars was dead. The Great War was over.

What the hell was Christine supposed to do now?

CHAPTER THIRTY-ONE

Ty Brooks, demon hunter extraordinaire, chased after his latest bond jumper. He howled with delight when he saw the ridge up ahead.

Got you now.

He'd traced this one to a world that appeared to be made out of limestone, yellow and crumbly. Weird columns of rocks were scattered throughout, a maze of great climbing routes. The air held traces of the many races who'd come here, either to climb or maybe to dive—the cliff edges loomed above deep ocean waters that were evidently gentle and full of amazing fish. It was a sort of vacation spot.

The demon Ty chased after couldn't swim, at least as far as he knew. Couldn't fly either.

Ty loped after the demon in his wolf shape. He rarely ever completely transformed. However, since teaching Tina how to control some of her inner urges, he'd come to the realization that he may have been a little too controlled recently, may have been too focused on the hunting and not on the living.

Particularly now that the war was over and the good guys had won. He regretted that he hadn't been the one to catch Lars, but he wasn't sorry the bastard was dead.

He howled again as he spied his prey, a sound guaranteed to send shivers down the spines of those creatures who had them.

The demon sent up his own howl in return. Instead of continuing to run, he stopped. Turned. Grew another set of arms, below the massive tube-like barrels coming out from his sides.

Oh shit.

Ty started shifting back into a semi-human state as he ran, a trick he'd only recently perfected.

By the time he reached the demon, he had his own sword drawn and was ready to use it.

"I'm here to take you back to the court!" Ty roared at the creature.

"So?" the demon challenged.

Ty came to a stop, his sword raised, ready to fight or dive to the side. "I'm not here to kill you," he said. "Just to take you back. But I will take back merely your body if that's what you insist on. Your choice how you return to the court."

The demon actually appeared to think about it for a moment. It was difficult to tell. It had three saucer-like eyes, each brimming with yellowish pus. Mottled green and yellow skin covered its muscular body, like a moss-covered rock. Its mouth was a nightmare of pointed teeth and forked tongues, three of them, in fact.

And now, it had six arms, each looking ready to tear Ty's heart out at the slightest provocation.

Luckily, Ty had been training. A lot.

He'd acquired two new students in the weeks since the war. While they'd both needed the meditations and mind practice, one had also needed more physical training as well.

Ty could see himself start to teach more. Maybe get Dennis to work up some advertising for him. Start off with enough students in the mornings to make it worth his while, and only go off chasing bounties in the afternoons and evenings. Slowly acquire more students, letting the teaching edge out the hunting, and eventually retiring.

Not today, though.

The demon nodded to itself after a bit, wiping some of the (surely poisonous) black ichor that had begun to drip down the side of its mouth. "Let's dance," he growled.

Ty couldn't help but grin as he raised his sword higher, prepared to fight.

What could he say? He loved his job.

CHAPTER THIRTY-TWO

DENNIS SAT IN THE DARK IN HIS LIVING ROOM, ON his comfy leather couch, drinking a beer. The windows of his condo showed the lights of downtown Bellevue, and behind him, clocks and other electronics glowed brightly.

He didn't normally sit in the dark, alone, drinking. In fact, the last time he'd done so had been just before he'd decided to turn over a new leaf, as it were. Become someone new.

It had been such an incredible turning point for him. That one single decision, to go and talk with the rowdy boys, instead of sitting and stewing when Christine was late for dinner.

He would consider it a defining moment for the rest of his entire life.

He'd thanked Christine more than once for giving him a chance. But here, in the dark, he was going to have to acknowledge that it hadn't been just her. She'd opened the door for him, yes. Shown him the way. However, he was the one who'd done the work. He'd made the choice, then continued to choose those things that would make him happy.

He could barely recognize the old him who'd been sitting on this very same couch less than a year ago.

He'd hate to admit it, but he might have finally started growing up. Sure, he'd thought that he'd been an adult before. That was before he'd started working for himself. No one to blame but him when things went sideways. No one to take the credit either.

He listened more than he ever had before, and he'd thought before that he'd been a good listener. Nope. There were still things he could do better there in that regard, he was sure of it. He had even considered getting one of those self-help books on it, or maybe taking a class on it.

He was also willing to ask questions when he was confused. Hell, he'd even ask for directions now. He couldn't fake it when it came to the *kith and kin*. Their customs, worlds, knowledge was just too different from his. He had to ask about things he didn't understand, admit his own ignorance. Be uncomfortable, and learn.

As a result…he'd found himself the perfect mate. Partner. Co-conspirator, though unindicted.

He raised his beer in a silent toast before he took another sip, grinning. He had to admit that Toby, the oracle, had been right in his initial judgment of Dennis. He hadn't been ready for Laurie at that point, hadn't been grown up enough.

Now though…It had only been a few weeks, but Dennis had already started thinking about what it would be like to have a wife. Kids, even.

Hell, go and buy a house in the suburbs instead of his slick condo in the city.

He shook his head and took another sip of beer. He couldn't believe how much he was looking forward to each and every day, how lucky he was, how grateful he was.

Yeah, Christine and Laurie were never going to get along. He winced when he thought about it. But Christine was willing to work on it, trying to meet Laurie halfway. And Laurie understood the difficulties, why the pair of them were never going to get along due to their basic natures, and was also willing to try.

Yup. Life was just going to get better and better, at least as far as Dennis could see.

Maybe he should start thinking about getting a ring…

He sat in his darkened living room, grinning, sipping his beer and feeling thankful for that one, singular decision. And how he was never going back.

CHAPTER THIRTY-THREE

Ozlandia sat in her office with the guard role books on her desk, waiting for the first visitors of the day.

When the king had ordered the guard back from the war, she'd had to strike so many names from the books that she couldn't get anything else done for a solid week.

Now that the war was over, some of the trolls were coming back, seeing if they still had a place in the guard. Not as many as she'd thought, however.

Seemed a lot of them decided to stay with their families instead. They'd earned their war scars and their stories, as well as a small pension. They didn't need anything more.

Ozlandia was looking forward to her routine returning to normal, whatever that would be. Sparring regularly with Kizalynn again, maybe. She didn't train new recruits—she'd break them if she tried, without meaning to. No, she regularly trained with the older trolls. She was only in her mid-forties, had never married and had no desire to have kids. Other trolls always said that she'd been born old, though.

Things still weren't right in the palace. Ozlandia remained loyal to the king, despite the fact that he was, well, aging before their eyes. Since the end of the war he'd gotten cranky. More like an old man.

What would she do when, not if, Kizalynn insisted that King Garethen step down? What would Ozlandia do? Who would she side with?

Luckily, that wasn't a decision that she had to make that day.

"Come in!" she called to the troll who'd just stuck his head into Ozlandia's office.

She had work to do, re-enrolling good, hard-fighting trolls in the king's guard.

And that had to be enough for now.

CHAPTER THIRTY-FOUR

Vern stood behind the counter at Nikolai's Emporium and Trade Goods, waiting. He'd thought about renaming the shop, but it hadn't seemed like the right thing to do. Not yet. He may rename it after a couple of years, though not after himself. "A Swell Place for Magic Goods" just didn't roll off the tongue, though he really liked that name, himself.

Lizzie sat beside him, reading a paperback. They'd discovered early on that human electronics didn't really work well in the magic shop, so she'd gone back to reading on paper, and always carried a book with her when they went to the shop.

Across the back of the shop, as well as just above Vern's head, were huge banners that announced the grand reopening of the shop. He'd set the portals to active that morning, ready to welcome everyone into his shop.

No one had come that morning.

Vern wasn't sure what to do about that. He wouldn't allow himself to be troubled about it. Not yet. It took time for word of mouth to get around, for the human magicians as well as some of the *kith and kin* to realize that the shop had reopened.

He'd let the human magical council know about it. He'd put out fliers in the council chambers, during their last meeting. He'd asked Christine to spread the word as she finished cleaning up a few remaining pockets of demons who hadn't immediately fled the worlds they'd been squatting on.

Now, all he had to do was wait. He'd built back up the stock, being careful to choose those items that, according to Nik's detailed records, had been popular. They would come.

A cool hand suddenly squeezed his, Lizzie reaching up to give him comfort. "It will be okay," she assured him.

He smiled down at her. "It'll be better than just okay. It'll be groovy. Just you wait and see."

Lizzie rolled her eyes at him then went back to her paperback.

A quiet *bing* intruded on Vern's consciousness. He'd worked with Malcom on getting the tone just right, so that Vern would always know when a being activated one of the portals to come into the shop. It wasn't an easy spell. Vern knew he'd have to tweak it some more, later.

But that first tone was so soft, so melodious, it started his heart to sing.

Customers!

Vern eagerly waited for the being to step through the opening at the back of the shop.

A single being walked through. Vern identified her as a pixie right away, based on her extraordinarily long fingers

—like sticks—her sharp pointed teeth, and hay-like hair, sticking out in all directions. She wore a simple cotton dress that hung on her gaunt shoulders like a garment on a hanger, bare skinny legs sticking out from underneath, and no shoes.

"Can I help you?" Vern asked in English, trying to sound friendly. He didn't know the native language of the pixies. There was a type of babblefish spell that he still needed to figure out, so that he'd always be able to converse in a being's tongue, but it was too advanced for him. Something to work on in a few years.

The lights, too, still needed work. Vern could automatically adjust the magical lights embedded in the ceiling to whatever level he liked. He hadn't yet managed the complicated spell that Nik had up, so the lights would change to the level of whatever the customer wanted.

There were just so many things to learn! To do! Vern was pretty sure he'd never get to even half of them, even if he lived to be one hundred and twenty, as he always threatened.

"Hi," the pixie said, sounding shy. "Uhm, you got any charm bags?"

"Sure," Vern said. "The bags are on the second shelf, down that aisle," he added, pointing. He gripped the counter with his other hand tightly to prevent himself from walking around it to show the pixie where the charm bags were kept. Everyone had told him to stay on *his* side of the counter if he wanted to keep his customers happy.

It grated on Vern that he couldn't be more friendly. Hopefully, as the years went on, he'd be able to be more "hands on" as it were with his regular customers.

Vern had used Nik's regular supplier for the bags. The retail price was cheap, though the bags themselves were made out of beautifully dyed heavy silk. Vern had also ordered a few of the fancier bags in the catalog, the ones with hand-sewn pearls and fancy brocade, just because they were so beautiful and he thought they might sell.

The pixie walked directly to the aisle. She picked up one of the fancier bags and studied it for a moment, before she put it back down and selected a deep red one from the basket of regular bags.

She spent a few moments perusing the rest of the stock there on the shelf. Vern had kept all of Nik's shelving units, as they'd been handmade by Nik and enchanted to be immune to any of the magical items that might be stored on them, so the magic wouldn't seep out and infect the wood.

Yet another thing that Vern had to learn—how to do that himself so he could keep the enchantments up.

"Is that all?" Vern asked, keeping his voice cheery as the pixie came up to the counter with the single bag. He'd really wanted more for his first sale.

Still. First sale!

Though the price had been clearly displayed on the basket, the pixie still immediately started bargaining with Vern. He allowed her to knock a third off the price, knowing that he was going to make more than double what the bag cost to purchase.

"Thank you for your business," Vern said as he collected her grubby change. "Be sure to tell all your friends about us, that the shop is open for business again."

The pixie nodded and sniffed absentmindedly. Then

she appeared to pause and think for a moment. "You don't need any help here, do ya?"

Vern blinked, surprised. That had been the absolute last thing that he'd imagined his first customer might ask about.

"I don't know," he said honestly. "The shop has just reopened and I really have no idea how busy I'm going to be."

The pixie nodded and looked sad. Then she got a sly smile. "Hows about I send lots of people here? Then you might need help?"

"Maybe," Vern said slowly, nodding.

How good would a pixie helper be? Did he want a helper? Could he afford to pay a helper?

She gave him a great grin. "I'm Latisha. You remember that. I'll come back in a week." Then she turned and walked back out the portal.

Vern turned in amazement to Lizzie, reaching out and squeezing her hand. "Our first sale!" he exclaimed, handing the (admittedly filthy) coins to her.

They'd agreed to keep the first few coins, maybe display them in a box, instead of spending them.

Lizzie smiled up at Vern. "And possibly your first employee."

"Kind of groovy," Vern said.

Lizzie merely nodded, tucked the coins away into her pocket, and went back to reading.

Kind of groovy indeed.

CHAPTER THIRTY-FIVE

King Garethen took his first sip of the most excellent beer at Tanner's Way. He hadn't come back to the bar since he'd been exposed as a royal, during that drunken dart game.

However, he'd found himself wanting to come back, at least one more time. Since his disguise was illusionary, he didn't have to appear as he had been. He did tone down the green of his skin and put gold caps on his tusks again. This time he'd really changed his facial features, making himself look much fatter than he normally did, with pudgy cheeks and a small, fat nose.

The barkeep still stared at him hard when he first ordered. She didn't say anything and she did charge him the "tourist" price. He still would bet that she had recognized him, as she kept shooting glances his way as he stood and listened to the usual quartet singing in the corner.

Ah well. Nothing to be done for it.

It was good for him to get out of the palace, though he

didn't really like to do it. The palace was the most comfortable place for him. Especially the closet where he kept the trunks of gold.

He knew they were infected with demon spells. He could handle it, though. Keep them shoved away, out of his thoughts, for most of the day.

It was only at night that it grew bad, that he almost felt as if they called to him. He never made decisions at night, as he suspected they wouldn't be sound. The rest of the time, he could fight the influence. He was sure of it.

So occasionally he slipped. Mostly he was himself. He didn't need to get rid of the trunks. Just the thought of doing so hollowed out his gut.

But he was in control. Really. Not them.

He'd even started handing over royal responsibilities to Kizalynn. Not that he was going to abdicate anytime soon. Maybe in a year or two. He'd also let his closest advisors know that he was thinking about it. They'd all said they thought it was wise.

Maybe then, he could come up with a different disguise. Make Tanner's Way a regular, weekly stop. The beer was sure worth it…

Garethen decided to stop after three beers. Not that he couldn't hold his liquor, but it would make him slower in the morning, when he was meeting with Kizalynn.

"Excellent as always, my dear," the king told the barkeep.

"It's always my honor to serve you," the barkeep replied quietly.

Only then did Garethen realize what he'd said, indicating that he'd tasted her beer before.

But she would keep his secret. That warmed his heart, which felt cold too often these days.

Garethen stepped outside the brightly lit tavern, ready to make his way back to the palace. He'd left a note saying where he was going, as always. He paused for a moment, waiting for his eyes to readjust. He had excellent night vision, as did most trolls, so he was surprised that it seemed to be taking some time.

"This way!" came a softly whispered voice.

Garethen looked to the right. He could vaguely make out the appearance of a troll.

A fog must have rolled in from the river. The air was cool, rapidly growing chilly. The smell of the nearby tanneries washed over him, the stench bad enough that he nearly gagged.

"This way!" came the urgently whispered words again.

Garethen squinted. It was a male troll calling him. He wondered if this was a trap. Did some robber think that Garethen made an easy target? He chuckled quietly. Wouldn't that be a surprise when they suddenly realized they were fighting a warrior and not a merchant?

Up ahead, the figure still appeared as just a dark outline in the fog. He had broad shoulders and walked with an easy gait.

Kizalynn had taught Garethen the human trick of carrying weapons in a hidden space around him. Quickly he drew out his ax.

Yes, these rogues would be in for quite a surprise.

Only when Garethen walked all the way behind the building and into the alley did the other troll show himself, stepping close enough that Garethen could see him.

Josekanly.

King Garethen felt torn. On the one hand, he still thought Josekanly was a fine young troll.

On the other hand, he remembered Kizalynn's assessment of the troll and his influences.

"What do you want?" the king asked, coming to a halt, keeping his sword at hand.

"Is that any way to greet your future son-in-law?" Josekanly said with a broad grin.

"What? What are you talking about?" Garethen said, confused. Had Kizalynn decided to forgive Josekanly and just forget to tell him about it?

Josekanly held up a contract. "It says right here that you've agreed to a merger between our two houses. The only way to do that would be through marriage." His face grew stern. "You don't know how you've hurt my mother by turning her away from the court."

"She hasn't visited the court in years," the king pointed out, still confused.

"Yes, but she was always planning on going back. You've taken away the one thing that was keeping her alive," Josekanly said. "She's slipping away now. Rapidly. You have to reconcile my family and yours."

"No, I don't," King Garethen said, feeling stubborn. "I'm sorry to hear about your mother, but there isn't anything I can do about that."

Really, what did Josekanly expect? That he could just order his king to do something?

"You have to sign this contract," Josekanly said. "This is the last time I'm asking. Please."

The king gave him a derisive snort. "Or else?" he challenged.

"Or else my friends will make you sign it for me," Josekanly said. He continued to hold the contract aloft while he took a step back.

A dozen demons materialized around Josekanly.

Garethen realized that the stench he'd thought had come from the tanneries down the block had actually been rolling off these beings. They were as tall as a troll, but thin and wiry. They had what looked like a duck beak sticking out from their faces, however their mouths were full of razor sharp teeth. Black and white spotted feathers covered their sleek heads, giving them a fast look. Their eyes were red and rimmed with layers of extra flesh, like built-in goggles.

Garethen knew that he could successfully fight off even as many as four of these beings at the same time. Possibly half a dozen.

Not a dozen.

"I won't sign," Garethen said firmly.

"But you will!" Josekanly said, giggling like a mad fool.

Garethen struck first, hard and fast, surprising the first demon with a solid slice across his stomach.

At least they didn't bleed acid, which many demons did.

Garethen pivoted and struck the next one, forcing all of them back while he took another step to the side.

If he had a building at his back, they wouldn't be able

to sneak up that way. One less direction that they could attack him.

The next two came at him simultaneously. He swung his ax vigorously, changing to a one-handed attack, while punching at the other demon.

He didn't like not being able to pivot and defend himself using the old troll form of fighting. However, all the guard trained to fight this way as well, either with a wall or beside another troll.

The next attacker scored a solid hit against Garethen, raking one arm from shoulder to wrist. He nearly dropped his ax in surprise.

Gods, that hurt.

Garethen shook his head and tried to clear his vision. He swung out with his ax again, taking down the next demon easily but missing the other.

He felt his heart rate suddenly slow down. The cool night grew warm. Sweat poured from him.

Damn it! He'd been poisoned.

"Now, turn this way," Josekanly commanded as the demons stepped back.

Garethen felt his treacherous head follow Josekanly's voice.

"Come closer," Josekanly said.

Garethen took one shuffling step away from the wall, though he willed his body to stay standing still.

He would *not* do this. No matter how Josekanly compelled him to obey. He would *never* sign that contract.

He tried to dig in his heels but he found himself moving forward still.

"Just a little bit more," Josekanly said, pen and paper in hand.

Garethen shook his head. He was better than this. He was not some fool to be tricked.

Except he had been tricked by the demons, hadn't he?

"Put down your ax," Josekanly told the king.

Yes. He could do that.

Garethen dropped his ax on the ground and took another shuffling step forward.

He hoped the darkness would hide his actions, how he dug out a handful of small, sharp rocks out of the bag that most trolls wore tied to their belts.

Garethen wished he could touch the solid earth one more time. Smell the fresh hay when it was first cut from the fields. Maybe even talk with Kizalynn, say goodbye.

He wasn't about to die alone and desolate, however, having betrayed his people. He would go out like a good warrior, fighting to the end.

After two more steps, Garethen knew he was close enough. Before Josekanly even knew what happened, Garethen threw the rocks in his hand directly at Josekanly's head.

The first two landed exactly where Garethen had aimed—striking Josekanly's eyes and blinding him.

The last shot was pure luck, but it landed exactly where Garethen had aimed, straight down Josekanly's throat.

The sound of choking filled Garethen's heart with glee even as the chill the demons carried with them washed over him as they drew nearer.

He couldn't defend himself from their claws, now. They would tear him to pieces.

From the choked scream beside him, he knew that Josekanly couldn't escape the demons either.

They would die together in this back alley near the tanneries, fighting demons.

As the night closed in, Garethen found he really didn't have any regrets.

It was time.

CHAPTER THIRTY-SIX

Buddy sat on his throne sideways, with his legs over one of the arms, sipping his beer morosely with the rest of the demons who'd gathered together in his court room.

The demons had lost the Great War. The princes of hell had declared the war lost when Lars had fled the field instead of staying and fighting Kizalynn and her human sister, Tina.

That Buddy may have influenced the vote had nothing to do with the truth of the matter. The rest of the princes had agreed with him.

Lars had failed. There was no greater sin among demons.

But Buddy hadn't wanted all the food and alcohol prepared for Lars' victory party to go to waste, so he'd thrown his own "losers" party. Lots of spicy tacos and stir fry, as well as beer. The champagne fountain stood empty —the suggestion to turn it into a chocolate fountain had appeared to be ill-advised in the end, as you apparently needed a different mechanism and Buddy couldn't be bothered with all the details.

Of course, Buddy was sad that the demons had lost the Great War. However, he had warned the other demons about putting all their faith in a single being. Sure, he'd been the first to put his troops on the line.

However, he'd also been the first to withdraw his approval.

Lars had just been far too distracted there at the end. More concerned with his own fete than with the war. Too involved with the creation of his legend rather than doing the deeds that would feed it.

Or at least that was how Buddy's PR team had been spinning it. Successfully, as well.

No one wanted to admit that they'd had hope, once upon a time. They were demons, after all.

Curled up at the foot of Buddy's throne, sleeping soundly enough to make small squeaking sounds, was a round ball of brown fur. It wasn't a purebred Pomeranian —it had some Chihuahua mixed in. When the puppy woke up, it would be a frenzy of energy again, until it reached its limit and fell back asleep, sometimes in mid-bounce.

The other princes of hell had all speculated which soul Buddy was using this particular torture on.

If they only knew…

Buddy had thought long and hard about what he'd wanted to do with Lars' soul once he'd come into possession of it (as he knew he would). Just imprisoning it, putting Lars into the standard torture pits, was a sure route to failure. It would give Lars too much time to start planning and plotting again.

The thought of Lars organizing all those lost souls into a rebellion had actually left Buddy in a cold sweat more than one night.

No, he needed to do something that would distract Lars, keep him occupied so he didn't just tunnel in on himself and make more plans.

Eventually Buddy came up with the idea of imprisoning Lars in the body of a dog. A small, yappy dog that, while smart, wouldn't be able to plot his way free.

In addition, Buddy had sweetened the deal. He'd promised Lars that, once a year, Buddy would allow him to take a different corporeal form. Lars would have twenty four hours to convince Buddy of whatever scheme Lars had hatched while imprisoned in the dog body, unable to order his thoughts, distracted by whatever shiny thing came his way.

Buddy figured that it would take Lars at least five years to hatch his new plan, then between five to ten years to make the plan palatable.

Buddy had all the time in all the worlds.

Lars, though, couldn't ever become that yappy or destructive, or Buddy would tear Lars' soul to pieces and scatter them in the deepest, darkest pits of hell, each fragment aware and never able to escape.

Buddy had figured that Lars the dog would also be a great device that he could use to torture his own minions, making them take the dog out for walks, cleaning up after the puppy's messes, and so on.

Win-win.

Buddy took another sip of his beer. Sure, he was sad that the demons hadn't really won the Great War.

However, Buddy had come out on top. Not necessarily smelling like a rose, but not reeking of his own farts either.

And wasn't that what mattered in the end?

CHAPTER THIRTY-SEVEN

Christine woke up cranky. She couldn't say why. It felt as though a huge weight had settled onto her shoulders during the night.

She pushed herself up to sitting and looked around her room. Everything looked the same. She was in her underground chambers on the human side of the fairy bridge. The room was nicely dark, with good solid earth walls. Her bed was a marvel of human engineering—she'd spent extra on a mattress that would fit her troll form, as well as be the perfect blend of both support and comfort.

After rubbing the sleep from her eyes, Christine sniffed. Nope. Nothing there except her own sweat (she really needed a shower, despite the fact that trolls didn't sweat like humans) as well as the faint traces of her coffee with honey that she'd made herself the night before.

Christine was still trying to find a routine, now that the war was over. She had originally thought she'd just go back to the life she'd had before the fighting, but that hadn't been satisfying. Sparring was no substitute from chopping an opponent's limbs from their body.

The troll inside her wanted more blood. Christine wasn't sure how to satisfy that urge, or if it would go away after a while.

Instead of pushing back the covers and racing into her day, Christine had the luxury of going back to sleep. She'd promised herself a week of doing nothing but sleeping once the war had ended, and she hadn't quite gotten to it yet.

But she needed a shower, and her stomach was already awake and demanding some food.

Maybe tomorrow.

Christine went through her new morning routine, starting with going through the troll fighting form. This morning she took it easy and didn't actually perform it with her ax, though she knew that Ozlandia would make her go through the form an additional time later when she found out.

It was a good way to get her muscles flowing as well as waking up her brain. After that she *really* needed a shower, as well as breakfast.

Christine made herself eat more slowly than she had been, actually tasting and enjoying her food instead of bolting it down so she could go and meet her generals, or get to the first battle of the day.

Afterward, Christine sat in her living room sipping her coffee and debating what to do next. Sitting and reading a book didn't sound appealing, at least not right then. This afternoon or later that night? Would be perfect.

What should she do instead? How was she going to fill her days now that she wasn't fighting all the time?

She still didn't have a good answer for that.

A walk sounded like a marvelous first deed for the day. Christine sent her senses upward, figuring out what it was like outside.

Ugh. The fall rains had finally started. It was cold and miserable. Not that Christine was all that affected by the cold anymore. That wasn't what she was in the mood for.

Maybe it would be nicer in Trollville…

Christine remembered that she'd promised herself a day of shopping once the war was over. She needed a new fall cloak, and her boots could really use some work. It sounded like a lovely way to spend the rest of the morning, to go shopping for a while, maybe get a snack in the marketplace, then perhaps go to the palace and visit with Garethen.

Christine knew that she'd never be able to completely counteract the demonic influence over Garethen, not while he still held onto those trunks of gold. However, she was making inroads with him, starting to turn his intentions back toward good.

It would be a slow process. Christine had more hope now that she'd succeed than when she'd first started. He still lied about the trunks, how much he needed them. It was as bad as any human addiction.

Christine had vowed that she wouldn't start regularly sleeping at the palace until after the king had gotten rid of the trunks. She had crashed there occasionally. She wasn't as sensitive as Ty, couldn't actually smell the demonic influence. Still, the knowledge that the trunks existed in the same general location as where she was sleeping made her too uncomfortable.

Instead of using the fairy bridge and walking into Trollville, Christine used a merchant portal that she'd found, that tradesmen used for their goods. Ozlandia had placed extra guards on it when Christine had discovered the amount of demon-influenced goods that were being displayed in the hall of viewing.

Christine stepped out from her front room into a bustling street. The sky overhead was a wan blue, with thin clouds stretched across it. The portal itself was located behind the main shops on Market Street.

Christine greeted the two guards as she strolled through. She'd seen them before at this same location, though Ozlandia did change the guards out often so that none of them would be tempted with bribes.

Carts gathered on the left, piled up with goods, waiting for their turn to use the portal later that afternoon. Mornings were for deliveries into the kingdom, afternoons were for deliveries out.

Christine took in a good lungful of fresh air as she strolled down the alley. She felt a small spike of envy as she saw all the merchants and the workers busily scurrying about their business.

She still had no idea what she was going to do on a daily basis. Or as Dennis might tease her, what she wanted to be when she grew up.

Dennis really had grown up and was becoming a fine young man. Not that there had been anything wrong with the goofball she'd grown up with. Dennis now had a calmness about him that reminded her of the older trolls she'd met. She'd never thought of him as flighty; however, he was grounded now.

His girlfriend left much to be desired, but Christine couldn't hold that against him. Laurie had some angel blood in her. Of course she'd seem perfect to Dennis.

Christine just hoped that they'd be able to make it work, despite their differences.

Dad was happy running his shop, even if he still didn't have a steady stream of visitors. It gave him something else to do as well, a focus for his energies. Mum was helping there part time, though they'd talked about hiring this pixie as well.

Everyone had settled into life after the Great War. Even Tina, who helped Ty with his students as well as continued her own studies, determined to become a golden wizard—some sort of human magical rank that Christine still didn't understand, even though Tina had told her about it three times now.

Christine stepped onto the main street and just paused, taking in the scene. The food market had many trolls in it, walking from stall to stall, picking up the ingredients for their meals that day. The smell of fried bacon caught her attention, but she wasn't really hungry. Maybe later.

Then she turned away from the food stalls and toward the parts of the market that had clothes. Now, where was that cloak store she'd seen an age ago?

As Christine walked, the trolls she passed would frequently bow their heads to her, though the few who recognized her did gasp.

Was it so unusual for someone in the royal court to go shopping for themselves?

A beautiful display of raw silk scarves caught Christine's attention. She didn't really need a new scarf. But the jewel colors were exquisite. She paused and glanced through the various options, debating with herself as to whether or not she really needed another scarf anyway, just because.

Suddenly, a loud horn echoed through the air. Christine recognized it as the horn the crier sometimes used to announce the king.

Wait, was Garethen coming into the market? He would never do something like that. He stayed hidden at the palace and only came out disguised.

Huh. Christine walked out from the stall and further into the street.

All the other trolls in the street had melted back from the center, leaving Christine alone in the center of the brick pathway.

She shrugged. The king's guard would recognize her when they turned the corner.

It wasn't the king, though. Ozlandia led the group of marching trolls. They all wore their dress uniforms.

Except…except why did each troll have a white band tied to their right bicep? And why were they carrying a standard with a white flag tied to the top of it?

Christine had won the Great War. This wasn't a sign of defeat, was it? What were they surrendering?

The procession stopped immediately in front of Christine. She had the feeling that they'd come looking specifically for her.

As one, all of the troll guard dropped to one knee.

What the hell?

Christine bit her tongue, though she wanted to tell them to rise up now and tell her what was going on.

All the trolls in the street grew silent. The only sound became the rustling of cloth as they all knelt as well.

Finally, Ozlandia looked up, directly into Christine's eyes.

"The king is dead," she called out in a loud voice that washed over not only this block but the ones beside it. "Long live the queen."

CHRISTINE DISMISSED THE GUARDS WHO'D FOUND the body of the king. She remained seated behind the desk in her study after they'd gone.

It had been a make-shift office for her during the war. Now, she was going to have to outfit it with decorations, shelves, a proper desk, visitor chairs—the whole works. She might even steal the king's huge purple geode, but it was too soon to think about that now.

She still didn't know what to make of the death of the king. He'd been found in an alley near the tanneries. Evidently he'd been to a tavern nearby, and had been there more than once.

That the king had been killed by demons didn't surprise her. It also wasn't terribly surprising that the body of Josekanly—Joe, the marketing troll—had been found beside the king.

Christine let it be known that the pair of them had

been attacked by the demons, who'd been looking to force the king into signing a contract, deeding the demons a permanent home in Trollville.

There wasn't anything she could do about the other rumors, particularly since some of them were true.

Chances were that Josekanly had brought the demons with him, as the other part of the contract had been asking for her hand in marriage. Strictly speaking, he'd probably been killed by the demons, though the way his eyeballs had been shattered suggested that he'd been hit by something first. Certainly looked like stones thrown by an angry troll.

Christine would never know. She suspected that her nightmares wouldn't be kind, though, and would show her Garethen gladly accepting the demonic influence just so he could marry her off.

There were so many things to do, now. So many things to plan for. The funeral would be the next day. Her coronation would take place the week after that.

She did have to laugh at herself from time to time, remembering that brief moment when she had nothing planned.

She didn't know when she'd ever have that luxury again.

Already, the various factions of the court were angling to get her to select their son for her mate. Christine wished that she had the excuse of running a war, but instead, had to go to all these social events instead. It was now part of her job, as Dennis had gleefully reminded her.

Seemed she had some more growing up to do as well.

At least Christine had been able to clean out the king's

private rooms. She'd brought in Ty as well as the Thothian to find and get rid of every piece of demonic influence.

It had broken her heart all over again when she'd realized that the king had stopped sleeping in his bed and had instead been curled up on the floor in front of the trunks of gold in that tiny closet.

At least he was at peace, now. And he'd gone out fighting. She would make sure that was how he'd be remembered.

For now, Christine had a kingdom to run. As well as a mate to find. Her thirst for blood had faded some. However, she now understood why trolls, even untrained trolls, made such fearsome warriors. Her own nature demanded battle and fighting.

It was just that now her battles would be in the court and not on the field.

So much to do. Less than when she'd been fighting, but still, every day was now full.

The future beckoned, bright and shiny now. Sure, she'd still have some dark times, nightmares of demons and her own failings.

However, she'd finally found her place.

Queen of the trolls did have a nice ring to it.

Now, she just had to find the perfect tiara…

READ MORE!

Be sure to read all the books in the Seattle Trolls series!

The Changeling Troll
The Princess Troll
The Fairy-Bridge Troll
The Troll-Demon War
The Troll-Human War
The Troll-Troll War

Available for sale now!

ABOUT THE AUTHOR

Leah Cutter writes page-turning fiction in exotic locations, such as a magical New Orleans, the ancient Orient, Hungary, the Oregon coast, rural Kentucky, Seattle, Minneapolis, and many others.

She writes literary, fantasy, mystery, science fiction, and horror fiction. Her short fiction has been published in magazines like *Alfred Hitchcock's Mystery Magazine* and *Talebones*, anthologies like Fiction River, and on the web. Her long fiction has been published both by New York publishers as well as small presses.

Find Leah's books here.

Follow her blog at www.LeahCutter.com.

Reviews

It's true. Reviews help me sell more books. If you've enjoyed this story, please consider leaving a review of it on your favorite site.

Come someplace new…

Are you a traveler? Do you enjoy exploring strange new worlds, new cultures, new people?

Sign up for my newsletter and I'll start you on your travels with a free copy of my book, *The Island Sampler*.

I will never spam you or use your email for nefarious purposes. You can also unsubscribe at any time.

http://www.LeahCutter.com/newsletter/

ABOUT KNOTTED ROAD PRESS

Knotted Road Press fiction specializes in dynamic writing set in mysterious, exotic locations.

Knotted Road Press non-fiction publishes autobiographies, business books, cookbooks, and how-to books with unique voices.

Knotted Road Press creates DRM-free ebooks as well as high-quality print books for readers around the world.

With authors in a variety of genres including literary, poetry, mystery, fantasy, and science fiction, Knotted Road Press has something for everyone.

Knotted Road Press
www.KnottedRoadPress.com